About Lucy King

Lucy King spent her formative years lost in the world of Mills & Boon® romance when she really ought to have been paying attention to her teachers. Up against sparkling heroines, gorgeous heroes and the magic of falling in love, trigonometry and absolute ablatives didn't stand a chance.

But as she couldn't live in a dream world for ever she eventually acquired a degree in languages and an eclectic collection of jobs. A stroll to the River Thames one Saturday morning led her to her very own hero. The minute she laid eyes on the hunky rower getting out of a boat, clad only in Lycra and carrying a three-metre oar as if it was a toothpick, she knew she'd met the man she was going to marry. Luckily the rower thought the same.

She will always be grateful to whatever it was that made her stop dithering and actually sit down to type Chapter One, because dreaming up her own sparkling heroines and gorgeous heroes is pretty much her idea of the perfect job.

Originally a Londoner, Lucy now lives in Spain, where she spends much of the time reading, failing to finish cryptic crosswords, and trying to convince herself that lying on the beach really *is* the best way to work.

Visit her at **www.lucykingbooks.com**

One More
Sleepless Night

Lucy King

First published in Great Britain 2013
by Mills & Boon, an imprint of Harlequin (UK) Limited.
Harlequin (UK) Limited, Eton House, 18-24 Paradise Road,
Richmond, Surrey TW9 1SR

© Lucy King 2013

ISBN: 978 0 263 23472 5

Also by Lucy King

The Couple Behind the Headlines
Say it with Diamonds
The Crown Affair
Propositioned by the Billionaire
Bought: Damsel in Distress

Did you know these are also available as eBooks?
Visit www.millsandboon.co.uk

For Emma

CHAPTER ONE

THERE WAS SOMEONE in the house.

With the slam of the front door ringing in her ears, Nicky sat bolt upright in bed, her heart hammering like a pneumatic drill, alarm racing along her veins and her fingers gripping the edges of her book so tightly her knuckles were white.

A couple of seconds ago she'd been lying back against the pillows, happily lost in the romantic world of *Don Quijote*. She'd been trotting across the dry deserted plains of La Mancha in search of knight errantry and adventure, and vaguely contemplating the intoxicating notion that for the first time in weeks she might actually be beginning to relax.

Then the door had slammed and she'd hurtled back to reality. All thoughts of fighting off imaginary giants had shattered. Any hope of tilting at windmills had evaporated. The sense of relaxation had vanished, and now every instinct she had was alert and quivering and one hundred per cent focused on the fact that *there was someone in the house.*

And not someone she knew, she thought, her brain galloping through the facts as her blood chilled and a cold sweat broke out all over her skin.

Because as much as she'd like to believe otherwise, there was no way the heavy footsteps stamping over the rough flagstones of the hall and echoing off the walls could possibly belong to Ana, the pint-sized housekeeper. Or Maria, the laid-back cook. Or any of the other staff employed on the estate for that matter. Some of them might be big and burly enough to possess a tread like the one now heading up the stairs, but none of them would be in this part of the house at this time of night.

No one was, apart from her.

And, of course, whoever it was who'd reached the landing, dropped something that hit the floor with a thud and was now striding down the long wide corridor towards her room.

Nicky's heart hammered even more fiercely and her blood roared in her ears as it struck her that the footsteps were getting louder. Closer. That any minute now they'd stop, he'd be at her door, the handle would turn and—

Images of what might happen then slammed into her head, vivid and terrifying, and as the alarm rushing around her turned to full-blown panic she started to shake. Her vision blurred, her breath stuck in her throat and she went dizzy, and her heart was now beating so hard and fast it felt as if it were about to burst from her chest.

She was a split second from passing out, she realised foggily, and then the panic exploded inside her because if she *did* pass out then she'd be toast.

And she really didn't want to be toast. She didn't want *not* to be able to find out whether she might actually be able to sort out the mess her life had become. She'd waited too long. Suffered too much. Tried too hard...

So no, she told herself, struggling through the haze in her head and battling back the panic. No way was she giving up now and no way was she fainting.

Dredging up strength from who knew where and taking a series of deep breaths, Nicky determinedly reined in her spiralling-out-of-control imagination and willed her heart rate to slow because she really had to calm down.

Now was *not* the time to lose it. Now was the time for cool assessment and a plan, because, regardless of what might lie in store for *her*, she was damned if she was going to let whoever it was get his grubby hands on her precious camera. Even if it had been sitting in a cupboard and gathering dust for the last few months.

Besides, she'd been in situations far more hazardous than this and had escaped at least *physically* unscathed so why should this be the one to get the better of her?

The most important question right now therefore was: what was she going to do? Simply lying here, frozen still and quivering with panic, wasn't going to get her anywhere, was it? Nor was dithering. No, it was time for action.

Allowing the instincts that had served her so well for so long to take over Nicky raced through the options. Options that weren't all that abundant, she had to admit, but never mind. She only needed one to work with and—aha!—now she had it. And in the nick of time, it seemed, because the footsteps had slowed right down and were a fraction of a second from stopping altogether.

Setting her jaw and clutching the book even tighter, she thanked God she'd picked an unabridged and illustrated copy of *Don Quijote* for her bedtime reading—which came in at a whopping thousand pages and weighed a ton—and silently slid from the bed.

What a week.

Striding down the corridor towards the sliver of light that shone from beneath the door at the end of it, Rafael rubbed a weary hand over his face and stifled a yawn.

He didn't think he'd ever had one like it, and frankly he'd be happy never to experience one like it again, because he couldn't remember a time when the muscles in his body hadn't ached or when his nerves hadn't been wound so tightly, let alone the last good night's sleep he'd had.

The crippling exhaustion could be attributed fairly and squarely to the merger he'd been working on recently and which had finally gone through this morning. It was a deal that had required delicate negotiation, tactful management, endless patience and long, long days at the office. All of which, of course, he'd been happy to handle. He was used to it, and sorting out other people's problems with their businesses was what he did best.

What he hadn't been so happy to have to deal with, however, and what was causing the unbearable tension in his nerves, were the myriad demands that the women in his life had chosen to unleash on him over the last few days.

Firstly, Elisa, the woman he'd been dating but had finished with a fortnight ago, had pitched up at his office the day before yesterday apparently unable to accept they were over. Despite the fact that he'd repeatedly pointed out he'd never promised her anything more than a casual fling, she'd been convinced she could change his mind, and the set of her jaw and the look in her eye had told him that no matter what he did or said she wasn't going to give up easily, as her subsequent battery of phone calls had proved.

Too busy and too knackered to deal with a full-on showdown right then and there, Rafael had sighed, muttered something about discussing it another time, and had eventually pacified her enough to bundle her out and send her on her way.

He'd barely got over *that* confrontation when his mother had been on the phone complaining about the fact that his father was once again holed up in his study and showed no signs of emerging. She'd demanded Rafael do something about it, although quite what she'd expected him to do he had no idea, because for one thing when his father retreated there was no shifting him, and for another he'd never paid his son any attention before so why would he start now?

When he'd eventually prised out the reason behind his father's withdrawal—the flap his mother was getting in over
the organisation of a charity ball months away—he'd told her
he could quite understand why his father had locked himself in his study, and that if it were *him* he wouldn't emerge
until the night of the ball was long gone. At which point his
mother had hung up on him in a fit of pique.

Then hot on the heels of *that* phone call, his eldest sister
had invited him to a dinner party she was holding tomorrow
night, which he suspected she'd engineered for the sole pur-
pose of lining him up with one of her many single friends.

Rafael did *not* need help with his love-life, as Lola was
well aware, but she'd inexplicably made it her life's mission
to see him hitched again. Which was a thoroughly futile ex-
ercise because he had no intention of ever remarrying, especially not to any of his sister's friends, given the traumatic
mess it had caused the last time he'd tried it. Once was quite
enough, as he'd told her on countless occasions, but Lola had
an infuriating habit of brushing him aside with a dismissive
wave of her hand, and it was getting to the stage where if
she didn't back off he might well lose it.

By the time his youngest sister, Gabriela, had begun her
relentless onslaught of phone calls and emails, in the inter-
ests of self-preservation Rafael had made the snap decision
to ignore her and everyone else, and flee the madness that
was temporarily defining his life.

Whatever Gaby wanted it could wait, he'd assured himself, jumping into his car and telling his driver to make for
the airport via a quick detour to his flat for a suitcase, then
hopping on his plane and heading south.

He'd done the right thing by escaping, he told himself
now. He'd known it the second he'd got out of his car a couple of minutes ago and for a moment had just stood there in
the inky velvet of the night, listening to the blessed silence,

breathing in the scent of earth and jasmine as the dry heat wrapped itself around him, and feeling some of the excruciating tension gripping his muscles ease.

Quite apart from probably collapsing with exhaustion, if he'd stayed in Madrid the usually strong bonds of filial and fraternal affection might well have snapped, so he refused to feel even a pinprick of guilt at disappearing without a word. His mother and sisters would survive perfectly well without him for a week or two. And as for his father, well, over the years he'd proved eminently capable of looking after himself by burying himself in his beloved books whenever there was a sudden surge of emotion about the place, as was being demonstrated by his current study sit-in.

So no. No guilt, he told himself, stopping at the door, wrapping his hand round the handle and turning it. He deserved a break. He needed one. All he wanted was a week or two of peace and quiet at the vineyard he'd had no option but to neglect for the last few months. He wanted long early morning walks among the vines and endless lazy afternoons drinking wine by the pool. He wanted rest and relaxation. Fresh air and sun and, above all, solitude. Was that *really* too much to ask?

Rafael opened the door a fraction to reach in and flip the switch he presumed had been left on by mistake, and his last coherent thought as the door slammed back, as something struck him hard in the temple, as pain detonated in his head and everything went dark inside as well as out, was that evidently it was.

Yes!

With a heady mix of adrenalin and triumph racing through her, Nicky heard the intruder groan, watched him stagger back in the shadowy darkness, and blew out the breath she'd been holding for what felt like hours.

Hah. That would teach whoever it was that she was not to be messed with. That she might be in a bit of a state at the moment, that she might be out here miles from anywhere and practically all alone, but that she was far from defenceless.

Her attack-being-the-best-form-of-defence plan had been an excellent one, and with the element of surprise on her side he hadn't stood a chance.

Still didn't by the looks of things, she thought with a surge of satisfaction as he swayed to one side, hit the door frame and, with a torrent of angry Spanish, ricocheted off it.

Oh, he didn't sound at all happy, but Nicky ignored the urge to wince and refused to feel guilty at the thought she might have done him some real damage because why should she when she was the potential victim here?

Not that she felt particularly victimish right now. In fact she'd never felt more victorious, which, after weeks of feeling nothing but listless, desperate and hopeless was very definitely something to be tucked away and analysed.

Although that analysis might have to wait until later, she thought, the satisfaction zapping through her slowly dissipating. Because with hindsight maybe her strategy hadn't been quite as brilliant as she'd thought.

He was filling the doorway and therefore blocking her only means of escape, and now, judging by the way he was giving his head a quick shake and straightening, he was making an alarmingly speedy recovery.

Her stomach churned with renewed panic as her mind raced all over again. Oh, heavens. If she wanted to leg it and make it to safety she was going to have to administer a second blow. One that would this time fell him like a tree and incapacitate him for the few minutes she'd need to clamber over him and run.

With barely a thought for the consequences and focused solely on survival, Nicky channelled every drop of adrenalin, every ounce of aggression she possessed, and raised the book again.

But before she could slam it down, he hit the switch, lunged forwards and grabbed her. Stunned by the sudden brightness of the light and by the sheer force of the bulk that crashed into her, Nicky let out a shriek and lost her balance.

As if in slow motion she felt herself go down. Felt her assailant follow her. Felt a large hand clamp onto the back of her head and a strong arm snap round her back. She heard the thud of the book as it landed on the carpet and wondered vaguely what she was going to do for a weapon now.

After what seemed like hours but could only have been a second, she hit the floor. Her breath shot from her lungs. Her vision blurred, her head swam and her entire body went numb. For a few endless moments the only thing she could hear was the thundering of her heart and a weird kind of roaring in her ears.

And then the dizziness ebbed and the shock faded and as feeling returned she became aware of the warm ragged breath on her cheek. Of the hammering of a heart against her chest. And of the very considerable weight half lying on top of her, crushing the breath from her lungs, pressing her into the floor and showing no signs of shifting.

Or of anything for that matter, she realised dazedly, which meant that she had the advantage and she had to use it. Now.

Preparing to knee him where it would *really* hurt and hoping that that might succeed where *Don Quijote* had failed, Nicky glanced up to get a good look at the man she'd need to describe to the police.

And froze, her leg bent slightly at the knee and her hands flat against the hard muscles of his shoulders.

She stared up into the face hovering inches above hers, up at the dark-as-night hair, the thickly lashed, startlingly green eyes, the deep tan and that mouth, all so exquisitely put together, the face she'd seen countless times in the photos on Gaby's mantelpiece—although admittedly never in its current furious state—and her breath shot from her lungs all over again. Only this time in one shuddery, horrified gasp.

The triumph vanished. The satisfaction disappeared. The thundering adrenalin and mind-scrambling panic evaporated in a puff of smoke. And in their wake came a flood of red-hot mortification.

Because, oh, dear God...

As unlikely as it seemed, and despite the fact that she'd been assured he was in Madrid and would never show up at the estate he'd lately abandoned, she'd just brained her host.

CHAPTER TWO

WHAT THE—?

WITH all the breath knocked from his lungs slowly return-ing, Rafael stared down at the figure sprawled beneath him barely able to believe his eyes.

This was the person responsible for the pain splintering his head apart and the juddering agony shooting up his arms from his wrists to his shoulders? This… This…*woman*?

Judging by the force of the blow he'd received he'd been expecting a six foot plus chunk of man, armed with a crow-bar and sporting a balaclava at the very least, which was why he'd retaliated so vigorously and lunged.

He would never in a million years have guessed that his assailant would turn out to be a woman probably two-thirds his size. Or that she'd have the long dark wavy hair that was fanning out over his hand and the floor and the big blue-grey eyes that were widening with shock and alarm and hor-ror. And he'd never have imagined that she'd be half naked.

Yet unless the thwack to his head was making him hallu-cinate, it appeared that, what with the long limbs entangled with his and the feel of her silky hair and soft skin beneath his hands, that was exactly the case.

Cross with himself for even noticing what she looked like and what she was—or wasn't—wearing when it couldn't have been less relevant, Rafael scowled, and since that made the pounding in his head worse he let out a rough curse. He felt as if someone were drilling a hole through his skull while repeatedly punching him in the stomach.

He hurt. Everywhere.

As must she, given that he was lying on top of her and probably crushing the life out of her, he thought, hearing her muffled groan.

She released his shoulders, let her knee drop and clapped one hand over her eyes, and he eased his arms away from underneath her, rolled off and lay back flat out on the floor. He closed his eyes and breathed in deeply in an effort to stifle the pain and try and make some kind of sense of the last couple of minutes, but it didn't work because none of this made any sense at all.

'Oh, my God,' said his assailant, her voice sounding hoarse with appal and breathlessness, and very English. 'I'm so *so* sorry. I had no idea... Are you OK?'

OK? Rafael wasn't sure he'd ever be OK again. If anything, the pain in his head was getting worse. What on earth had she lamped him with? Surely not just a fist. If that was all it had taken he was in a worse state than he'd imagined.

'Rafael?' This time her voice was lower, softer, more concerned. Sexier, he thought, and got a bit sidetracked by the image of the two of them lying not on a cold hard stone floor but a soft warm bed, wearing considerably less clothing, with that voice whispering hot filthy things in his ear.

And then she gave him a decidedly unsexy little slap on the cheek.

Rafael flinched as the erotic vision vanished, and refocused. God, she'd just attacked him and he was *fantasising* about her? What was his problem?

And what was *her* problem? Wasn't practically knocking him out enough? Had she really had to slap him too? What did she have lined up next? A methodical and thorough assault of his entire body?

Vaguely wondering what he'd ever done to womankind to deserve this torment on top of everything else he'd had to endure lately, he gingerly opened his eyes.

And saw stars all over again because she was on her knees, leaning over him, and he was getting an eyeful of creamy cleavage. So close he could make out a spatter of faint freckles on the skin of her upper chest. So close he could smell the delicate floral notes of her scent. So tantalisingly close all he'd have to do was lift his head a handful of centimetres and he'd be able to nuzzle her neck.

At the thought of *that*, his mouth watered, a wave of heat struck him square in the stomach and for the first time since she'd hit him he forgot about the pain throbbing away in his temple. The image of the two of them in that bed slammed back into his head, more vivid than before now that he had more detail to add, and he blinked at the intensity of it.

'Thank God,' she murmured, letting out a shaky breath, which made her chest jiggle and his pulse spike. 'Are you all right?'

How he managed it he had no idea but Rafael made himself drag his gaze up and look into her eyes. Eyes that were filled with worry, set in a face that was pale and, he thought, letting his gaze roam over it, perhaps a bit thinner than it ought to be.

There was nothing thin about her mouth, however, he decided, staring at it and going momentarily dizzy as a fresh burst of heat shot through him. Her mouth was wide and generous and very very appealing, especially what with the way she'd caught the edge of her lower lip between her teeth and was nibbling at it.

'Ow,' he muttered, forcing himself to remember the faint sting of the slap because the alternative was yanking her down and giving in to the temptation to nibble on that lip himself, which was so insanely inappropriate given the circumstances that he wondered if the blow to his head might not have done him a serious injury.

'I'm sorry—again—but I thought you'd passed out.'

'I'm fine,' he said, although actually nothing could be further from the truth, because now he was imagining that mouth moving over his, then pulling away and sliding over his skin, hot and wet and sizzling, and the throbbing in his head was breaking loose and rushing down his body with such speed and force that he had the horrible feeling that when it got to his groin he might do exactly as she'd feared and pass out.

He lifted his hand to his temple and touched it, as much to see if she'd drawn blood as to find out whether deliberately and brutally provoking pain might dampen the maddening heat.

'Do you think you might be concussed? Should I get help?'

'No, and no,' he said irritably because while on the upside she hadn't on the downside it didn't.

'Let me take a look.'

Before he could stop her she'd leaned down and reached across him and was now sifting her fingers through his hair. Her breasts brushed against his chest, then hovered perilously close to his mouth, and the heat churning through him exploded into an electrifying bolt of lust.

God, what the hell *was* this? he wondered, bewilderment ricocheting around his brain. Since when had he reacted so violently to a woman he'd barely met? And since when had he had to fight so hard to keep a grip on his supposedly rock-solid self-control?

'Leave it,' he snapped and wrapped his hand round her wrist to stop her going any further.

To his relief she went still, then frowned and, as he let her go, mercifully straightened and sat back. 'Well, if you're sure.'

Rafael hitched in a breath, briefly closed his eyes and ordered himself to get a grip before he embarrassed himself. 'I'm sure.'

With what felt like superhuman effort he levered himself upright and set about engaging the self-control he'd never had such trouble with before. He drew his feet up to hide the very visible evidence of the effect she'd had on him, rested his elbows on his knees, and began to rub the kinks out of his neck with both hands. He let out a deep sigh. So much for peace, tranquillity and nice quiet solitude.

'I really am sorry, you know,' she said, her voice sounding rather small.

'So you said.'

'I thought you were a burglar.'

'If I was, I wouldn't be a very good one,' he muttered, remembering the way he'd slammed the front door and thundered up the stairs in his haste to crash out and wipe the last week from his brain. 'I wasn't exactly subtle.'

'Well, no,' she admitted, 'but at the time a cool, logical analysis of the situation wasn't uppermost in my mind. I acted on instinct.'

And how he'd suffered for it. Her instincts were so dangerous they should come with a warning.

As should that body. Because she might have backed off but she was still far too close for his comfort. She was now kneeling beside him and sitting back on her heels and her smooth bare thighs were within stroking distance. At the thought of sliding his hands up her legs, his fingers itched and he dug them just that little bit harder into his neck.

'The next time I come across a closed door,' he said, setting his jaw and trying not to think about silky thighs and itching fingers, 'I'll knock.'

She nodded. 'Probably a good idea.'

'All I thought I was doing was simply switching off a light that had been left on by accident. Who knew helping the environment could be so lethal?' He glanced at the book lying innocently on the floor behind her and frowned. 'What the hell did you hit me with?'

'Don Quijote,' she said, wincing and going pink.

That would certainly account for the bruise he could feel swelling at his temple. 'I always thought that book was utterly deadly,' he said darkly, 'but I never thought I'd ever mean literally.'

'You were supposed to be in Madrid.'

At the faint accusatory tone of her voice his eyebrows shot up. 'Are you suggesting that this,' he said, breaking off from massaging his neck to indicate his head, 'is somehow *my* fault?'

She frowned. 'Well, no,' she said, sounding a bit more contrite and biting on that damn lip again. 'But if you'd been expected I imagine Ana would have warned me and then I'd have been listening out for you instead of attacking you.' And then she lifted her chin and pulled her shoulders up and back, which did nothing to help his resolution to keep his eyes off her chest. '*Were* you expected?'

No, his decision to come down here had been uncharacteristically on the spur of the moment, and with hindsight that might have been a mistake, but that wasn't the point. Rafael arched an eyebrow and threw her a look that had quelled many a thick-headed CEO. 'I wasn't aware I needed to be.'

'No, of course you don't,' she said, flushing a bit deeper. 'It's your house. Sorry.'

And that was the third time tonight she appeared to be one step ahead of him, he thought with a stab of annoyance.

In addition to taking him by surprise earlier, she apparently knew his name and that this was his house. Whereas he knew nothing about her apart from the fact that she was probably British, looked incredibly hot in her skimpy T-shirt and knickers and had skin and hair that felt like silk beneath his hands. The latter two of which, he reminded himself for the dozenth time, weren't in the slightest bit relevant.

Giving himself a mental slap, Rafael pulled himself together. He'd had quite enough of being on the back foot for one evening. Quite enough of having his nice ordered life being thrown into increasing disarray. It was high time he asserted some kind of control over this particular situation at the very least, and focused on what was important.

'You're right,' he said coolly as he fixed her with his most penetrating stare. 'So perhaps you wouldn't mind telling me who you are and what you're doing here.'

She blinked at him for a moment or two, then gave him a tentative smile. 'Well, I'm Nicky.'

She said it as if it should have been obvious, and Rafael frowned. 'Nicky?'

'Sinclair.'

He racked his brains for a spark of recognition but came up with nothing. 'Is that supposed to mean something?'

'I was rather hoping so.'

'It doesn't.' He was pretty sure he didn't know any Nickys, Sinclair or otherwise, and equally sure he didn't want to if they were anything like this one.

'Oh.'

Her smile faded and something tugged at his chest. Rafael ignored it and concentrated on his original line of questioning. 'And what are you doing in my house?'

'I'm here on holiday.'

His eyebrows shot up. Since when had the *cortijo* been open to visitors other than his family? 'On holiday?'

'That's right.'

'How long have you been here?'

'Two days.'

'And how long were you planning to stay?'

She shrugged then looked uneasy. 'Well, I don't know. I hadn't really thought.'

Hmm. He really ought to have made more of an effort to come down here over the last few months, tricky merger or no tricky merger. In the five years he'd had the place he'd generally managed to make it down once a month, but lately he'd been so tied up with work he'd had no option but to stay in Madrid. He'd received the usual weekly reports about the vineyard, of course, but heaven knew what had really been going on in his absence.

'Are there any more of you?'

She looked at him warily. 'No, just me.'

That was something to be grateful for, he supposed, shoving his hands through his hair before he remembered the bruise, and grimacing as a fresh arrow of pain scythed through him.

It shouldn't be too hard to get rid of her. His plane was sitting at the airport a mere half an hour away and could take her anywhere she wanted to go at a moment's notice. Within the hour he could be enjoying the solitude he'd been hankering after.

There was no question of her continuing her holiday, of course, because quite apart from the fact that the house wasn't open to visitors—of either the paying or non-paying variety—none of his fantasies about escaping everything for a few days had featured a hot house guest with a penchant for violence.

Besides, he'd finally reached the end of his usually fairly long tether, and he'd had enough. Of everything. So he'd send Nicky on her way, wipe the bizarrely traumatic events of this evening from his memory, and set about relaxing.

But not while they were both still on the floor, he decided, getting painfully to his feet then holding out his hand to help her up.

'You have absolutely no idea about any of this, do you?' she said a little wistfully as she put her hand in his and stood up.

'No,' he muttered, so disconcerted by the sizzle that shot through his blood at the contact that for a second he had no idea about anything.

'I knew it would turn out too good to be true.'

She sighed, slid her hand from his and Rafael ignored the odd dart of regret to focus instead on the way her shoulders were slumping. 'What would?' he asked, detecting an air of defeat about her and for some reason not liking it.

'Coming to stay. Gaby said it would be fine.'

That captured his attention. 'You know Gaby?'

She nodded and gave him another wobbly little smile. 'I do. And she said she'd clear it with you, but she didn't, did she?'

That would teach him to issue an open invitation to his sisters to use the place whenever they felt like it. Rafael thought of the barrage of phone calls and emails that his sister had bombarded him with and which he'd disregarded, and frowned at the niggling stab of guilt. 'No.'

'I thought not.' She sighed again and seemed to deflate just that little bit more.

He watched it happen and to his intense irritation his chest tightened. There was a vulnerability about Nicky that plucked at the highly inconvenient and usually extremely well-hidden protective streak he possessed. Which was nuts, of course, because presumably the kind of woman to wallop him over the head as she had wasn't in the least bit vulnerable. Or in need of protection.

Nevertheless, right now she looked crushed, as if she had the weight of the world on her shoulders, and Rafael found he couldn't get the words out to tell her to leave, however much he wanted to. Besides, if she was a friend of his sister's and he threw her out, he'd never hear the end of it.

He sighed and inwardly cursed. 'Look, it's late,' he said, deciding that he was way too tired for this kind of mental gymnastics and as it was pushing midnight he could hardly turf her out now anyway. 'Let's discuss this in the morning.'

'OK,' she said, with a weariness that made him want to do something insane like haul her into his arms and tell her everything was going to be all right. 'Thanks... And goodnight.'

'Goodnight,' he muttered, then turned on his heel and strode off down the corridor, thinking with each step that the night had been anything but good so far, and what with the traces of arousal and heat still whipping around inside him and the apparent disintegration of his brain it didn't look as if it were going to get any better.

Well, this was all just typical of the crappy way her life had been going lately, wasn't it? thought Nicky glumly, watching Rafael stop to pick up the suitcase he must have dumped at the top of the stairs earlier and then disappear round the corner.

Why would her stay at the *cortijo* be turning out as she'd hoped when nothing had done recently?

Feeling utterly drained by the events of the last half an hour on top of those of the past six months, she shut the door, retrieved *Don Quijote* from the floor and padded over to the bed. Setting the book on the bedside table, she slipped beneath the sheets and switched off the light.

How had things gone so badly wrong? she wondered for the billionth time as she stared into the darkness and felt the relentless heaviness descend.

Six months ago she'd been unstoppable. So full of energy and verve and enthusiasm, and fiercely determined not to let what had happened in the Middle East defeat her. She'd snapped up every assignment she'd been offered and had thrown herself into each one as if it were her last. She'd travelled and worked every minute she had, pausing only to hook up with the scorchingly hot journalist with whom she'd been having a sizzling fling.

Everything had been going marvellously, exactly as she'd planned, and she'd enjoyed every minute of it. She'd taken some of the finest photographs of her career and had some of the best sex of her life, and she'd congratulated herself on beating any potential demons she could so easily have had.

See, she'd told herself on an all-time high as she collected an award for one of her pictures and smiled down at the man she was sleeping with. All those colleagues who'd muttered things about PTSD had been wrong. Apart from the occasional nightmare and a slight problem with crowds, she hadn't had any other symptoms. And besides, she wasn't an idiot, so as a precaution she'd embarked on a course of counselling and therapy, which had encouraged her to make sense of what had happened, and get over it. As indeed she had, and the full-to-the-brim life she'd been leading, the work she'd been doing and the award she'd won, were all proof of it.

For months she'd told herself that she was absolutely fine, and for months she'd blithely believed it.

Until one day a few weeks ago when she turned out to be not so fine. That horrible morning she'd woken up feeling as if she were being crushed by some invisible weight. Despite the bright Parisian sunshine pouring in through the slats in the blind and the thousand and one things she had to do, she just hadn't been able to get herself out of bed.

She'd assured herself at the time that she was simply having a bad day, but since then things had got steadily worse. The bad days had begun to occur more frequently, gradually outnumbering the good until pretty much every day was a bad day. The energy and verve and the self-confidence she'd always taken for granted had drained away, leaving her feeling increasingly anxious, and to her distress she'd found herself refusing work she'd previously have jumped at.

Bewildered by that, she'd stopped picking up her phone and had started ignoring emails. And not just those from colleagues and employers. When staying in touch with friends and family had begun to require too much energy she'd stopped doing that too.

She'd given up eating properly and had started sleeping terribly. When she did eventually manage to drop off the nightmares had come back, but now with far greater frequency than before, leaving her wide awake in the middle of the night, weak and sweating and shaking.

Her previously very healthy libido had faltered, withered and then died out altogether, as, inevitably, had the fling.

Barely going out, hardly speaking to anyone, and with so much time on her hands to sit and dwell, Nicky had ended up questioning practically every decision she'd ever made over the years. She'd begun to doubt her abilities, her ideals and her motivation, and as a result cynicism and a bone-deep weariness had invaded her.

Down and down she'd spiralled until she'd been riddled with nerve-snapping tension, utter desolation, crippling frustration, and the dizzyingly frightening feeling that she might never be able to haul herself out of the slump she tumbled into.

Burnout, Gaby had diagnosed over a bottle of wine a

week ago when Nicky had finally hit rock bottom, although what made her such an expert she had no idea. Gaby, who was currently feng shui-ing the mansion of a businessman in Bahrain, was an on-and-off interior designer—more off than on—and wouldn't know burnout if it came up and slapped her in the face.

Nevertheless, as she'd sliced through Nicky's symptoms, and then relentlessly gone on about the importance of balance and rest and looking at things piece by tiny piece, Nicky had decided that perhaps Gaby might have had a point, which was why when her friend had come up with a plan she'd so readily and gratefully agreed.

Go to Spain, Gaby had said. *Get away from it all. Take some time out and restore your equilibrium. Rest. Sunbathe. Get a tan. You can recuperate at my brother's house. He's never there so you can stay as long as you need. Don't worry about a thing. I'll sort it all out.*

At the time Gaby had made it sound so easy, and, as she hadn't exactly had any ideas of her own, she'd booked a flight the following morning, buoyed up both by the thought of having something to focus on other than her own misery and at the heady feeling that *finally* she might be about to see the blurry flickering light at the end of a very long, very dark tunnel.

And OK, in the two days she'd been here she hadn't noticed much of a difference to her emotional state, but she knew she needed time at the very least.

Time it looked as if she wasn't going to get, she thought now, her heart sinking once again as she sighed and punched her pillow into a more comfortable shape, because it was blindingly obvious that Gaby hadn't managed to sort anything out, and it was equally blindingly obvious that, despite her friend's breezy assurances to the contrary, she wasn't welcome here.

Nicky closed her eyes and inwardly cringed as the image of Rafael's handsome scowling face drifted into her head. Quite apart from the initial burglar/assault misunderstanding, throughout the whole subsequent conversation they'd had he'd been tense and on edge, and had looked so mightily hacked off that she'd got the impression that he really resented her being there. Which meant there was no way she could stay.

If she did—and that was assuming he didn't chuck her out in the morning—*she'd* feel like the intruder, and she had quite enough on her plate already without adding guilt to her ever-increasing pile of problems.

So who knew whether the peace and tranquillity of the *cortijo* might have eventually worked their magic? Whether a couple of weeks of enforced rest and relaxation might not have been just what she needed? She wasn't going to get the chance to find out because one thing she'd learned from years of working in hostile environments was never to hang around where you weren't welcome.

Therefore no matter how depressing she found the idea, first thing in the morning she, her suitcase and her nifty little hire car would be off.

CHAPTER THREE

DESPITE HIS MISGIVINGS about any improvement to his night, he'd actually slept remarkably well, thought Rafael, smothering a yawn and setting the coffee pot on the stove.

When he'd eventually made it to his room after leaving Nicky, he'd downed a couple of painkillers and then taken an ice cold shower, which had respectively obliterated the pain throbbing in his head and the heat racing through his veins. He'd crashed into bed and had been asleep barely before his considerably less painful head had hit the pillow. Consequently he'd woken up in a much better mood.

Back in full possession of his self-control and all his faculties, he'd had ample opportunity to assess the events of the previous night and had come to the conclusion that he'd overreacted. Big time. He'd been tired and overwrought. In pain and on the defensive. All entirely unsurprising of course given the circumstances, but nevertheless he *had* overreacted.

For one thing, he told himself, lighting the gas ring beneath the pot and straightening, he doubted that Nicky, with her big blue eyes, tumbling dark curls and long slender semi-naked limbs, could be nearly as distracting as he'd imagined last night, and the cold light of day would soon prove it.

His reaction to her last night might have been startling, but it was nothing to get worked up about. Any red-blooded heterosexual man would have responded like that to a gorgeous near-naked woman practically draped over him. It would have been unusual if he hadn't.

Nor were the oddly erotic images that had peppered his dreams anything to worry about either, because that was just his subconscious processing what had been an unexpected and surprisingly traumatic half an hour.

For another thing, last night he'd somehow managed to see Nicky as some kind of threat to his peace of mind, which was a sign of just how tired and at the end of his tether with women he'd become because the very idea was ridiculous. Since his divorce he'd made sure that no woman—apart from family members, and he couldn't unfortunately do much about them—had ever had such an effect on him, and a woman he barely knew certainly posed no risk.

The second conclusion he'd come to was that there was no earthly reason Nicky couldn't stay. Why they both couldn't. The place was big enough, and however exhausted and fed up he was it wasn't Nicky's fault. Nor was it her fault that he'd ignored Gaby's phone calls and emails and was therefore unprepared for a guest. And yes, she'd lamped him so hard it would have made a saint curse the heavens, but perhaps that was understandable in the circumstances.

Besides, he couldn't get the image of her standing there enveloped by that air of defeat and desolation out of his head, and it had been niggling away at his brain all morning. For someone supposedly on holiday Nicky didn't look very happy. And who holidayed by themselves anyway? Not even he did, and he valued his solitude highly.

Rafael poured some milk into a jug and stuck it in the microwave, then leaned back against the rough wood worktop and rubbed a hand along his jaw as he contemplated the contradiction.

He supposed Gaby might have been able to shed some

light on the situation if he'd been able to get hold of her, but her phone had been off all three times he'd tried. And the emails and messages he'd eventually got round to checking had said nothing more than 'call me' with varying degrees of urgency.

But that didn't matter. He didn't need to speak to his sister to recognise that there was more to Nicky and her 'holiday' than met the eye. In fact, he'd repeatedly gone over the way she'd deflated right there in front of him and got the feeling that she was in some kind of trouble. And if that *was* the case, then despite the fact he had no interest in—and even less intention of finding out—what kind of trouble she might be in, he'd never forgive himself if he sent her on her way and something subsequently happened to her.

So she was going to have to stay.

Which was absolutely fine, he assured himself, hearing a strange rumbling making its way across the floor above and abandoning the coffee to go and investigate. He had plenty of things to be getting on with, and staying out of Nicky's way while she got on with whatever she was planning to do would be simple enough.

And if he *did* still feel a lingering attraction towards her, well, he'd easily be able to handle that too. After what he'd had to contend with lately, suppressing tiny pangs of inconvenient desire would be a walk in the park. Especially now that he was well rested, firing on all cylinders, and most importantly, firmly back in control.

Leaving might be the right thing to do, thought Nicky as she trudged along the corridor hauling her suitcase behind her, but it didn't make it any easier, because what was she going to do when she got back to Paris?

Moping around her flat didn't particularly appeal. Neither did booking another holiday and having to go through the whole packing/airport/people thing again. And she supposed she could track down her parents and see if they needed any help, but right now their relentless cheerfulness might be more than she could stand.

Oh, if only Rafael hadn't chosen this of all weekends to visit… If only Gaby had managed to get in touch with him… If only she hadn't bashed him over the head…

If only…

Her spirits sank even further. There'd been so many 'if only's in her life lately. She'd never used to believe in regrets, and she'd never used to wish for the impossible. However since her meltdown it seemed she'd done nothing but, and she was becoming thoroughly sick of it.

Nicky gritted her teeth and yanked her suitcase over the edge of the rug that the wheels were rucking up. She *had* to stop all this before she lost what was left of her sanity. She really did. Regrets and impossible wishes and 'if only's were pointless, especially now, because there was nothing to be gained from wishing she could stay, and even less from dwelling on what might have been. However hard she might find it, she *had* to drag herself out of the past and start thinking about the future.

'Good morning.'

At the sound of the deep voice rumbling through her gloomy ruminations, Nicky came to an abrupt halt and stared down. Rafael was standing in the doorway to the kitchen, barefoot and rumple-haired, wearing khaki shorts, a black polo shirt and the kind of lethal smile that had undoubtedly brought about many a swoon but left her depressingly unmoved.

'Good morning,' she replied, despite thinking there wasn't much that was good about this one.

'Did you sleep well?'

Not particularly, but at least she hadn't had that hideous

recurring nightmare. 'Like a log,' she said, mustering up what she hoped might pass for a smile and feeling faintly glad there were no small children around to scare. 'You?'

'Beautifully.'

'How's the head?'

'Much better.'

That was one less thing on her conscience at least. 'Thank goodness for that.'

'It had more to do with paracetamol than goodness, but it's fine.' His gaze shifted to her suitcase and he arched an eyebrow. 'Going somewhere?'

Nicky bit back a sarcastic comment about his spectacular powers of observation because her frame of mind this morning was hardly his fault, and settled for the more boring but less offensive truth. 'The airport.'

'Oh?' he said mildly. 'Why?'

For a moment she just stared at him. Why? *Why?* Had a good night's sleep somehow wiped the previous evening's events from his memory? 'Because I don't fancy the long drive home,' she said, this time unable to hold back the sarcasm.

Rafael merely shrugged and grinned. 'Then stay.'

Nicky went still and blinked down at him, confusion stabbing at her brain. Maybe she'd misheard him or something. Or maybe she was hallucinating, conjuring up the words simply because she wanted to hear them. Whether she'd misheard or was imagining things, she definitely had the sensation that she'd woken up in some kind of parallel universe, because the Rafael who was leaning nonchalantly against the door frame, folding his arms over his chest and smiling up at her, bore little resemblance to the extremely grouchy man she'd met yesterday. *That* one had looked as if he just wanted her gone, so who was *this* one who was now suggesting she stay?

'What?' she said weakly, as a tiny ray of hope that she might not have to leave after all flickered through her bewilderment.

'Stay.'

'Really?'

He nodded. 'Really.'

The hope surged for a second and then stopped, hovered, and, because such good fortune didn't happen to her these days, the cynicism that was never far away swooped down and crushed it.

Nicky frowned and narrowed her eyes. Such a volte-face? Just like that? She didn't think so. 'Why?'

Rafael lifted his eyebrows. 'What do you mean why?'

'Last night I rather got the impression I wasn't very welcome.'

'No, but then you'd just hit me over the head. I wasn't in a very hospitable mood.'

She tilted her head and shot him a sceptical look. 'But this morning you are?'

'Apparently so.'

'Have you spoken to Gaby?' If Gaby had told him why she was here, then maybe he'd changed his mind out of pity.

'No. I tried, but her phone was off.'

'I didn't have any luck either,' she said, mightily relieved that Rafael didn't know the truth because the last thing she wanted was pity. 'She seems to have gone AWOL.'

'Probably sensible given the conversations I imagine she can expect.'

'Probably.'

There was a pause, then he said, 'So would you like to stay or not?'

Nicky bit her lip and scoured his face, but found nothing there to suggest he was anything other than one hundred per cent serious. She saw nothing but warmth in the depths of his eyes and in his smile, and felt a reciprocal stab of warmth in the pit of her stomach. Totally unexpected and alien, but so welcome it gave her the strength to push the cynicism aside for once.

Oh, what was the point of dithering any longer? Of course she was going to stay. There was trying to do the right thing and then there was being a stubborn idiot. Besides, she could stand there and try and figure out Rafael's motivations for hours, but she doubted she'd ever succeed and frankly she didn't have the energy for it.

And anyway, did it really matter why he'd changed his mind? No. All that mattered was that he was offering her the lifeline she hadn't realised she so badly needed until it looked as if it had gone, and she'd be a fool not to grab it with both hands.

'Are you sure I won't be a bother?'

'Quite sure.'

'In that case,' she said, feeling the beginnings of what she thought might be the first genuine smile to curve her mouth in months, 'I'd be delighted.'

CHAPTER FOUR

In his conviction that sharing his house with Nicky would present no problem he'd been one hundred per cent right, thought Rafael as he lit the barbecue later that evening. Handling his house guest and, more importantly, his response to her, was simply a question of remaining in control, and so far he'd been doing splendidly.

He could easily have let himself be swayed by the glorious sight of her on the landing this morning, but had he? No, he had not. He'd been ice cool. Unflappable. And as strong and steady as the Rock of Gibraltar that reared out of the sea a hundred kilometres to the south.

The flash of heat that had shot through him when he'd clapped eyes on her striding along and dragging her suitcase behind her, looking strangely and grimly determined, was merely down to the sky-high temperatures of Andalucia in August. Never mind that the sun had only been up for half an hour; the heat started early down here.

Throughout their subsequent conversation his grip on his self-control had only got firmer.

He'd barely noticed that her strapless dress was the exact colour of her eyes, clung to her curves and showed off inches of flawless skin. He'd paid no attention whatsoever to the way the sun pouring in through the window behind her rendered the skirt of her dress practically transparent and revealed the legs that had featured so prominently in his dreams.

When she'd slid her gaze to his temple and asked him how it was the sensation that he could somehow feel her fingers sifting through his hair again had been nothing more than a figment of his imagination. When he'd watched her nibble on that lip of hers and had felt a sharp twist of his stomach, it had had more to do with a hunger for breakfast than that of any other kind.

And if, when she'd agreed to stay and flashed him that sudden dazzling smile, he'd thought he'd gone momentarily blind, it was undoubtedly down to more of the eye-wateringly bright sunshine spilling in through the window.

Even now, with her sitting at the wrought iron table on the terrace, wearing a halter-neck dress that gave her a cleavage like the Desfiladero de los Gaitanes gorge he'd abseiled down last summer and the scent that had so intoxicated him last night, he was utterly unfazed. The tiny nick he'd given his finger when she'd tasted the wine and let out a soft little sigh of appreciation and the knife he'd been using to slice off a couple of steaks had slipped didn't hurt in the slightest.

Yes, he'd done well indeed, he told himself again as he sprinkled salt onto each of the steaks and then added a grind of pepper. Spending much of his day out in the fields among the grape-laden vines—not in an effort to avoid her or anything, of course, but because he'd needed to catch up with his estate manager—had clearly done the trick. Whatever attraction he'd felt for Nicky last night, whatever mental wobble he'd suffered, he'd most definitely conquered it, and he was well and truly back on track.

Rafael Montero really was the best looking man she'd seen in a long time, thought Nicky, lifting her glass to her mouth and watching him as he deftly flipped the steaks and seasoned the other side.

Last night and this morning she'd been on too much of an emotional roller coaster to appreciate his rugged good looks, and anyway, after grabbing a coffee he'd pretty much vanished until now so she hadn't really thought about it. But after spending the day reading by the pool she felt more relaxed and more aware of her surroundings than she had in months, and now he was right there in front of her—and now she was looking—she could well see his appeal.

Taking a sip of wine and savouring the cool crisp flavours that rippled over her taste buds, she let her gaze drift over him with the detached appreciation of the photographer she was.

He had the kind of height and breadth that made her own five feet seven now rather gaunt frame feel unusually small, thick dark hair that was made for ruffling, and a pair of shoulders that looked strong enough to bear all manner of burdens. His back was broad and beneath the white T-shirt that stretched across it she could see his muscles flexing as he moved.

She leisurely lowered her gaze down over his waist, his very fine bottom and long tanned legs, and then let it wander back up again. There was an air of tightly controlled restraint about him, a latent strength and power, and she had a sudden memory of that body lying on top of hers, heavy and hard and strong...

Oh, what a crying shame her sex drive was all out of batteries, she thought dolefully as she watched him slowly turn round and give her a view of his front, because he really was magnificent.

If only she'd met him a year ago...

Nicky hadn't exactly bed-hopped before she'd hit the doldrums but she'd always liked men. She'd loved the thrill of new attraction and the whole host of possibilities it opened up, in particular that of hot delicious sex with men she respected and admired but could leave without a twang of the heartstrings.

So if she'd met Rafael a year ago she'd have flirted like mad and after gauging his amenability to the idea would probably have set about seducing him into her bed.

Not so now, though, because as she completed her perusal of his spectacular body and found herself looking into that gorgeous face once again did she feel even a glimmer of a spark? A tingle of lust? A flicker of heat? No, she did not, which was depressing in the extreme because if a man like this didn't do it for her, then who would?

Nicky stifled a sigh and lifted her glass to her lips again.

'Have you quite finished?'

The dry tone of Rafael's voice made her jump, and she coughed and spluttered as the wine went down the wrong way. And then she went bright red because, regardless of how she did or didn't feel about him, it was still mortifying to have been caught ogling him.

'Yes. Sorry,' she gasped, clasping a fist to her chest and giving it a good thump.

'Are you all right?'

'Wine,' she managed by way of explanation, and cleared her throat. 'I'm fine.'

He picked up a bowl from the table beside the barbecue, brought it over and set it down in front of her. 'Have a prawn.'

Nicky wasn't sure having a prawn was all that advisable when she'd evidently lost control of her oesophagus, but took one anyway. 'Thank you.'

She dipped it into the little pot of aioli, then sucked it into her mouth and opened her eyes wide in delight as the juicy taste of the sea and salt exploded on her tongue. 'Wow, these are amazing.'

'Local,' Rafael muttered, his gaze on her mouth and his jaw tightening. 'Expensive.'

She smiled. 'But worth every *céntimo*.'

He didn't say anything, just kind of growled and shrugged and continued to stare at her mouth.

A funny tense kind of silence stretched between them and Nicky was beginning to wonder whether she might have a blob of aioli on her lip or something, when Rafael suddenly frowned, gave himself a quick shake, then threw himself into the chair opposite her.

'So how has your day been?' he asked rather more curtly than she thought the question deserved.

'Idyllic,' she said, swiping a paper napkin from the box to wipe her fingers and dabbing her mouth just in case, and telling herself that she must have imagined the flash of tension and the curtness because as far as she could see there wasn't anything to get tense or curt about. 'Ghostly pale isn't really me so I've decided to work on my tan. Me and my bikini barely moved from the pool all day.'

A muscle started hammering in his jaw and she thought she heard him grit his teeth. 'Sounds great,' he muttered.

'It was,' she said, briefly wondering if his obvious displeasure was down to her hogging of his pool. 'Do you mind?'

'About what?'

'Me monopolising your pool.'

'Not at all,' he said, lifting his gaze back to hers and giving her a tight smile. 'Make yourself at home.'

'Thank you,' she said, and, unable to fathom what the inscrutability of his demeanour was about, decided to continue with the small talk he'd initiated before any more of that weird uncomfortable tension had the chance to return. 'And how has *your* day been?'

Rafael rubbed the back of his neck, let out what sounded like a deeply exasperated sigh and sat back. 'Fruitful.'

'In the literal or metaphorical sense?'

'Both.'

'How come?'

'I spent the whole day with my estate manager discussing plans for an early harvest.'

'I imagine you must have had a lot to catch up on.'

Rafael arched a quizzical eyebrow. 'Why would you imagine that?'

'Gaby said you haven't been here for months.'

'I haven't.'

'Why not?' It seemed a shame when the place was a little slice of heaven on earth.

'I've been busy with work.'

'And now you're less busy?'

'For the moment.'

'So you're on holiday too?'

The minute the words were out of her mouth Nicky wished she hadn't brought up the subject of holidays, because as Rafael fixed her with that startling green gaze of his and leaned forwards she had the feeling that she might be about to regret it.

'I suppose I am,' he said. 'And talking of holidays...' He paused and she automatically tensed because judging by the probingly intense way he was looking at her there was no 'might' about it. 'Tell me more about yours.'

'What about it?' she asked and inwardly winced at her faintly prickly tone.

'You're here by yourself.'

'Evidently.'

'And indefinitely.'

'Is that so surprising?' Her fingers tightened around the

stem of her wine glass as she wondered where he was planning to go with this.

He tilted his head and regarded her for a second. 'I suppose not, but don't you have work to get back to?'

She forced herself to relax before her defensive air piqued his evident interest in the reasons for her 'holiday' even more. 'Not right now,' she said, deliberately breezily. 'I'm freelance.'

'In what field?'

'I'm a photojournalist.'

'What do you specialise in?'

Not a lot at the moment, she thought darkly, and decided to focus on the Nicky of a year ago rather than the wreck she was at the moment. 'Human interest stuff mainly. Droughts. Conflict. Public protests. That kind of thing.'

'It sounds dangerous.'

Nicky shuddered as the incident that had sparked off the traumatic chain of events that had led her here flashed through her head. 'It can be. On occasion.'

'So why do you do it?'

Wasn't that the million dollar question? 'Because I love it,' she said, channelling her old self and dredging up the motivation and beliefs she'd started out with. 'I love the idea of capturing a split second in time for ever. The look on a face, the mood of a crowd...' She stifled another shudder. 'I know it's a cliché but I really do believe that a picture is worth a thousand words. I also believe in the justice of it, in showing people the truth and the story behind the headlines.'

Or at least she had done. Now, though, she wasn't sure what she loved about her work or what she believed in. 'Plus I'm good at it,' she added, because it was high time she started thinking positively.

'I'm sure you are,' he said, breaking eye contact to take

a prawn of his own and toss it into his mouth. 'How did you get into it?'

Released from that probing gaze, Nicky felt as if she'd been holding her breath and had just remembered to let it out. 'I entered a picture in a competition when I was ten and won,' she said, giving herself a quick shake to dispel the light-headedness.

'Impressive.'

'I was addicted. I entered a lot of photos to a lot of competitions.'

'And what did you win?'

'A then state-of-the-art SLR.'

'And it all went from there?'

She nodded. 'That camera became my most treasured possession.' A snapshot of her young self with the camera inevitably hanging round her neck flashed into her head and a wave of nostalgia rose up inside her. 'I took it everywhere with me. I'd spend hours just sitting and watching the light and even longer making pretty much everyone I came across pose for me. I must have irritated the hell out of them... Anyway,' she said, dragging herself out of the past and back to the present, 'eventually I went to journalism college, got a couple of assignments and things kind of took off after that.'

'That simple?'

She shook her head. 'No. Actually it took years and it was incredibly hard work.'

'It sounds fascinating.'

She sat back and lifted her eyebrows. 'Does it?' For her the fascination had worn off a while ago.

'To a mere businessman like me it does.'

Nicky's eyes widened and her jaw dropped at the understatement. 'A mere businessman? You?'

Rafael raised his eyebrows and lifted his glass of wine to his mouth. 'What's wrong with that?'

'Nothing. But from what I've heard there's nothing "mere" about you at all.'

He went still, his glass hovering an inch below his lips and his eyes fixed on her with a disconcerting intensity. 'Why? What have you heard?'

Heavens, what hadn't she heard? Beneath the full force of his unwavering gaze Nicky fought the urge to squirm—and where had *that* come from anyway?—and considered what she'd learned about him. Given that she and Gaby had been neighbours for two years, and close friends for the last one of those, she'd learned plenty.

She'd heard that Rafael was some kind of corporate troubleshooter and that he was brilliant at everything, whether it was business, languages or women. She'd learned that he was thirty-two, a control-freak workaholic who didn't know when to stop, and that he'd had a brief but disastrous marriage. She'd also discovered that, despite his apparently innate talent for identifying and fixing problems, much to Gaby's and her sisters' frustration, he channelled this talent into his business, and steered well clear of entangling himself in any trouble that might involve his siblings.

Not that she'd be spilling all that out, of course. If anyone revealed that they knew so much about *her* she'd have had them arrested on the grounds of an invasion of privacy. 'Oh, this and that,' she said vaguely, aware that he was waiting for an answer.

'So you and Gaby haven't been discussing me?'

He looked so unexpectedly and endearingly put out by the idea that Nicky found herself in the unusual position of grinning. 'Well, you may have come up once or twice in conversation.'

He grimaced. 'I don't know whether to be flattered or worried.'

'You should be flattered.'

The grimace eased. 'Why? What did she say?'

'That you're a corporate troubleshooter and you like solving problems,' she said, deciding that if she condensed the facts it wouldn't sound too stalkerish, and actually feeling relieved to be talking about him rather than herself. 'That you're very driven and that your successes are stellar, both with work and with women.' She paused and then added, 'Oh, and that you're divorced.'

Rafael winced and she instantly wondered exactly what had gone wrong with his marriage. 'So perhaps not quite so successful with women.'

Telling herself that she had no business wondering and even less asking when they barely knew each other, Nicky tilted her head and had to agree. 'No, perhaps not.'

'Gaby has been chatty,' he said dryly, twisting the stem of his wine glass between long brown fingers.

'She's fond of you. And proud.'

Her heart squeezed in the same way it had done every time Gaby had either sung her brother's praises or lamented his failings.

She really ought to be used to it by now because, while the envy she felt at Gaby and Rafael's evident closeness had taken her by surprise at first, she'd lived with it for as long as she'd known her neighbour. If anything, though, instead of lessening the envy had grown and, the more she'd listened to Gaby, offering words of either awe or sympathy depending on the circumstances, the more she'd come to realise that she didn't have anyone who knew her or whom she knew quite that well. And in the early hours of the mornings when she'd been unable to sleep she'd begun to wonder if she might not be in the state she was in if she too had had someone that close to turn to.

'It must be nice to have siblings,' she said a little wistfully as the image of a two-point-four family popped into her head.

'Don't you have any?'

'Nope,' she said, pulling herself together because there she went again, wishing for the impossible. 'It's just me and my parents.'

'Lucky you,' he muttered, then got up and headed to the barbecue.

As she watched him slap the steaks on the grill Nicky frowned. She'd always got the impression from Gaby that while there was frustration aplenty between the sisters and their brother there was also a lot of affection. 'Really?'

She heard him sigh. 'No, not really,' he said, leaving the steaks to sizzle and spit on the grill and returning to the table. 'They're fine. Except when they're hassling me.'

'Do they do that often?'

'More often than I'd like,' he said, sitting back down and taking a mouthful of wine.

'So what do you do about it?'

'Well, the last time it happened I came down here.'

The tone of his voice made her insides cringe. 'Which was when?'

He set his glass down and gave her a look. 'Yesterday.'

Oh, dear. 'Looking for a bit of peace and quiet?'

He nodded. 'Only to be attacked with *Don Quijote*.'

Nicky felt her cheeks flush with mortification. 'I really am sorry about that, you know.'

'Don't worry, it was infinitely less traumatic than the quadruple whammy of one mother, two sisters and an ex-girlfriend.'

As her blush receded Nicky resisted the urge to roll her eyes because if *that* was what he considered traumatic he should try what she'd been through in the last six months. She'd take a mother, two sisters and an ex over the ghastly effects of burnout any day. 'Which was highly traumatic, I imagine,' she said as sincerely as she could, which wasn't very.

He raised an eyebrow at her arch tone. 'It seemed so at the time. Especially on top of such a busy time at work.'

Nicky reined in her cynicism because everyone had their hangups and actually what made hers any worse than his? 'Do they often gang up on you?'

'My sisters?'

She nodded.

Rafael tensed a little and her curiosity rocketed. 'Not since I was about eight.'

'Why? What happened when you were eight?'

'I chose not to let it bother me.'

The words were spoken casually enough but she caught the almost imperceptible tightening of his jaw and for some bizarre reason her heart squeezed again, only this time she didn't think it was with envy. 'Did it work?'

'Beautifully,' he said dryly, and gave her an easy smile that thankfully made the squeeze release its grip on her heart. 'Trying to rile someone who won't be provoked isn't much fun. They very quickly lost interest and left me alone.'

'Ingenious.'

He shrugged. 'Not so much ingenuity as a need for self-preservation. Anyway it worked because we now get along pretty well.'

Fleetingly wondering if choosing not to let things bother him was a strategy he still employed to deal with difficult situations, but realising that there was no way she could ask such a personal question, Nicky decided it would be safer for her heart and its surrounding muscles to move on to more neutral ground. 'So what does corporate troubleshooting involve?' she asked, toying with her glass as the mouth-watering scent of sizzling steak drifted towards her.

'I sort out companies in difficulties.'

'What sort of difficulties?'

'Anything really. A board might have a problem with

staffing or be going through a tricky merger or there might be issues with the management. I go in wherever I'm needed and leave when I'm done.'

'So you fix things.'

'I do.'

'Have you ever failed?'

'Not so far.'

'Do you fix people too?' she asked as it suddenly occurred to her that he might be able to fix her. And then almost as quickly she dismissed the idea as ridiculous because, for one thing, why would he want to help her when he didn't even get involved with his sisters' problems? And for another she was pretty sure that no one could fix her but her.

He shuddered. 'Absolutely not.'

'Why not?'

'Because it would inevitably get…emotional…and therefore messy.'

'And you don't do emotion or mess,' she said with a nod because the way he'd hesitated, the way he'd just flinched, said it all.

'Not if I can help it.'

As Nicky wasn't particularly fond of either, emotional detachment when it came to personal relationships was something she could definitely identify with, but nevertheless… 'Not even for your sisters?'

'Especially not for them.' He frowned. 'I wouldn't even offer them advice.'

'Really?' she asked, becoming increasingly intrigued by these insights into family life because as an only child she knew nothing about the dynamics of siblings, and with parents who championed independence she'd become so self-reliant she couldn't remember a time she'd asked for advice about anything.

'Absolutely. If the advice I hypothetically gave them was

wrong I'd invariably end up being blamed and if it wasn't taken then what would be the point of giving it in the first place? It would be a no-win situation, not to mention an insanely frustrating one.'

There was a certain amount of logic to that, Nicky supposed, and frankly what did she know about how families worked? 'Do they often ask you for advice?'

'They've learned not to,' he said darkly, and rose to head over to the grill to flip the steaks.

'Well, I don't know about the others, of course,' she said, remembering the long conversations during which Gaby had bemoaned her brother's lack of emotional support, 'but I think Gaby might appreciate being able to ask from time to time.'

Rafael turned and shot her a humourless smile. 'Gaby's the worst. She once asked me for advice years ago, which I gave her. She didn't take it and when things didn't work out she still blamed me.'

'Oh.' That Gaby had failed to mention. 'What happened?'

'You'll have to ask her. How long have you known her?' he said, coming back to the table and reaching for the bottle that sat in the middle of it.

'Two years.'

He poured her some more wine. 'Well, wait another thirty and then you'll see.'

'I'll bear it in mind.'

'How did you meet anyway?'

'She lives next door to me.'

His eyebrows lifted as he topped up his own glass, then sat down. 'In Paris?'

'That's right.'

'Yet you're British.'

And Gaby was Spanish. So what? 'It's a great place to be

based for the work I do,' she said, and told herself she really had to stop being so absurdly defensive. 'And yes, technically I'm British but I prefer to think of myself as a citizen of the world.'

He shot her a quizzical glance. 'Rootless?'

Hmm. Nicky tilted her head and pondered the question. She was certainly free and footloose. But rootless? She'd never really thought of it like that, but maybe Rafael was right because she'd been on the move for as long as she could remember.

Her parents had travelled extensively throughout her childhood—and still did—and she'd always gone with them wherever they'd been. As a result she'd never really had a base. She'd certainly never had a family home, or, come to think of it, a home of her own since. Even the flat she lived in now, with its minimalist décor and sparse furniture and general air of transience, was rented.

In fact the most permanent thing in her life was the suitcase she'd lived out of for the last ten years, a suitcase that was extremely well travelled and very battered but hanging in there. A bit like her, really.

'Perhaps,' she said, dragging her thoughts back on track and coming to the conclusion that Rafael was right about her lack of roots. 'And delighted to be so,' she added firmly, because that was about the only thing about her that hadn't changed in the last six months and it seemed important to remember it.

'Really?'

She nodded. 'Absolutely. I get itchy feet if I hang around in one place for too long. And the idea of staying in one place permanently...' She shuddered. 'Talk about stifling.'

'How come?'

'A by-product of my upbringing, I imagine.'

'Which was?'

'Internationally varied. My parents are anthropologists. They were—and actually still are—always heading off to investigate long lost tribes and things in far-flung places, and more often than not I accompanied them.' She paused and tilted her head. 'Remember that winning photo I took?'

Rafael nodded.

'It was of a Yanomami child. The Yanomami live in the Amazon rainforest,' she added in response to the quizzical look on his face. 'I was nine when I took it and it wasn't my first time in Brazil either. In fact, by the time I went to boarding school at the age of eleven, I'd got through three passports.'

'You've had an exciting life.'

She shrugged and felt her smile fade because lately it hadn't seemed quite so exciting. 'I've been lucky.'

There was a second or two of silence while he just looked at her and then he said, 'And yet with all that excitement you choose this place for a holiday?'

The words might have been spoken softly, but that didn't stop Nicky tensing. And it didn't stop a dart of wariness from flickering through her, because there it was again. The flash of perception—so similar to his sister's—in the dark green depths of his eyes, which told her that if she wasn't careful he'd be able to see far more of her than she wanted him—or anyone else—to.

'Well, why not?' she said, knowing she sounded on edge but feeling too unsettled to do a thing about it.

'It just seems a little sedate for someone so adventurous and globetrotting, that's all.'

Sedate was good, she thought, and determinedly pulled herself together. Sedate was exactly what she needed, so there was nothing wrong with sedate.

'Yes, well, adventure isn't always all it's cracked up to

be,' she said with as breezy a smile as she could manage, 'and sometimes even the most globetrotting of globetrotters needs a break, so thank you for inviting me to stay.'

CHAPTER FIVE

ALLOWING NICKY TO stay was the worst decision he'd made in years, thought Rafael grimly, staring out into the inky darkness of the night. What on earth had he been thinking? Had he *completely* lost his mind?

So much for all that peace and tranquillity he'd been after. And so much for all that rest and relaxation he'd hoped for. He'd never felt less peaceful, less tranquil, less rested or less relaxed. In fact, he was even more tense now than when he'd arrived and it was all entirely down to his unwanted house guest and the startlingly dramatic, insanely irritating effect she seemed to have on him.

How he'd ever managed to convince himself that he wasn't aware of Nicky he'd never know. Not aware of her? Hah. That was a joke. He must have been mad to even think it because over supper it had become pretty bloody obvious that he'd never been more aware of anyone, so since when did he do such complete and utter self-denial?

Rafael grimaced and knocked back another inch of his brandy. And to think that he'd blithely assumed he was doing so well. That his legendary self-control was fine. God, he was a stupidly arrogant idiot because he hadn't been doing well at all. He'd been doing dismally, and he hadn't even realised it.

He should never have suggested supper. If he'd known

what torturous agony *that* was going to be he'd have gone straight from the vineyards to his bedroom and stayed there until he was sure the coast was clear, but that was what hubris and the cook's weekend off could do to a man.

As a result, he'd had the most uncomfortable couple of hours he'd had in years, starting with the odd prickling he'd felt all over his skin when he'd been seeing to the steaks and had become conscious of the fact that Nicky was watching him.

He'd slowly turned, thinking that she might be mortified into jerking her gaze away, but was she? No. Those enigmatic blue-grey eyes of hers had continued to travel over him, languidly and totally unashamedly, and he'd been pinned to the spot, his body going into sensory overdrive and his head swimming.

But even then he'd just about held it together. Until he'd hit upon the idea of offering her a prawn in the foolhardy hope that moving on to food and small talk was the best way forward, and it had all gone downhill from there.

The prawns had been *such* a bad idea. There she'd sat calmly sucking them down and letting out those little soft moans while talking about her work, his siblings and her upbringing, and with every passing minute his head had got fuzzier and his body had wound tighter.

With his head filling with images of what Nicky might look like in nothing but a bikini as she lay by his pool, his stomach had twisted and his pulse had picked up until the desire he'd persuaded himself he'd conquered had slammed back with a force that had nearly floored him, and as hard as he'd tried he hadn't been able to stamp it out.

God only knew what they'd talked about after that because as night had descended he'd fallen more and more under her strangely hypnotic spell, until all he'd really been able to focus on was the way her mouth moved when she talked, the auburn streaks in her hair that the soft flickering candlelight picked out, and her funny little wistful smile.

Thank heavens she'd got up and announced she was off to bed when she had because he hadn't been sure how much longer he'd have been able to resist the growing pressure of desire.

It was completely baffling, he thought now, scowling down into his unexpectedly empty glass. He'd known her for less than twenty-four hours so how had things got so bad so quickly? When exactly had Nicky got into his head? And more importantly when exactly was she going to do the decent thing and get out? Because he really didn't want her in there.

For one thing, he absolutely did *not* need the hassle of a new affair so hot on the heels of the last disastrous one and, for another, what on earth was the point of wanting her when the attraction was so clearly one-sided?

Rafael set his glass on the table and let out a low growl of frustration. He'd had more than enough experience to recognise the signs of mutual physical attraction, and Nicky hadn't displayed any of them at any point. Which he should have been fine with, seeing as he was no longer a hormone-ridden teenager but a mature rational man of thirty-two, so the fact that he *wasn't* apparently fine with it annoyed him even more.

What *was* going on? And what the devil was he going to do about it?

He leaned forward to pour himself another brandy with which to contemplate the dilemma, but he'd barely reached for the bottle when a yell tore through the warm still night.

The shock of it made his heart lurch and his arm freeze in mid-stretch, and the anguish in it made goosebumps break out all over his skin. All thoughts of unrequited lust fled from his head and instinct took over.

Shoving his chair back, Rafael leapt to his feet, his heart thundering and adrenalin pounding through his veins. He wanted to race indoors and charge up the stairs. He wanted to fling back the door to Nicky's bedroom and see if she was all right. He wanted to find out why she'd yelled, what was wrong with her, and why she was really here. He wanted all that with such sudden clamouring urgency that every inch of him was tense and tight, poised and ready to—

He froze in his tracks as reason suddenly swooped down and barged aside instinct, and his blood ran cold.

God, what the hell was he thinking?

No. Absolutely not.

He didn't *do* concern. He didn't *do* rushing to the aid of damsels whether in distress or not. And he definitely did *not* want to know what was wrong with Nicky or what had caused her to cry out.

He shoved his hands through his hair and swore beneath his breath. He hadn't been lying when he'd told her he didn't sort out other people's personal problems. He might have grown up constantly being told by his mother that as their only brother he had a duty to protect and look out for his sisters, but he'd never met a group of girls who needed looking out for less. And the women he'd met subsequently—bar one—only confirmed the conclusion he'd reached that the so-called fairer sex was emotionally far tougher than the men he'd come across, and more often than not didn't appreciate help with any issues they might have.

Steeling himself against the lingering urge to act on his instincts and go and check on her regardless, Rafael set his jaw and made himself sit down. Whatever was plaguing Nicky was none of his business, and whatever had made her yell like that was probably nothing but a bad dream. Besides, it wasn't his job to fix her, and judging by her defensiveness

when they'd been talking earlier he doubted she'd appreciate the interference.

So he was doing the right thing by leaving her alone, he
assured himself as he splashed some more brandy into his
glass. Nicky would be fine, and come the morning he'd have
forgotten all about it so there was absolutely no need to give
it any further thought.

Sitting back and downing half his drink, Rafael resolutely
put it out of his head and turned his attention to his vines.

Nicky woke up a second before she cracked her head on the
tarmac. As usual.

Once again she'd been trapped in the midst of a swirling
mass of humanity, the bright colours blurring her vision,
the thunderous noise deafening her and the increasing air
of menace intensifying the panic and fear rocketing through
her.

Once again she'd lost her balance and had desperately
tried to counteract the momentum of the crowd by grabbing
at air, at anything really, but with the crush of people pressing in and around her it was to no avail. And once again
she'd felt herself go down and had filled with the sickening
heartbreaking awareness that once she hit the ground she'd
never get back up…

At least she hadn't cried out, she thought, staring blankly
up into the jet black darkness of the night, her heart pounding, sweat pouring off her and her head swimming with the
horrible images that *still* haunted her sleep.

As mercies went it was a small one, but it was a mercy
nevertheless because she knew from past experience that she
was perfectly capable of letting out a yell that could wake the
dead. Or, at least, Gaby, who'd pounded on her door often
enough, demanding to know if she was all right.

If she'd yelled out this time Rafael would undoubtedly

have heard and very possibly would have rushed in to see what was wrong. So it was a relief she hadn't because she really wasn't up to explaining.

Willing her heart to steady and her breathing to slow, Nicky sighed and flung an arm over her eyes and reminded herself for what felt like the billionth time that the shakiness and the fear pounding through her would pass. As they always did.

But, God, she was sick of the whole sodding lot of it. She was sick of the lack of control she had over her subconscious, sick of the hold that something that happened months ago still had on her—and her inability to get over it—and sick of being so prickly and defensive all the time.

It had to stop. Today. Now.

But how?

As the turbulent images faded and her trembling stopped something Rafael had said earlier flickered through her head. Something about not letting things bother him. Or rather, about *choosing* to not let things bother him…

Well, that was what she'd do too, she thought with grim resolution, because she had a choice, didn't she? Maybe not about what went on while she was asleep, but while she was awake? That was a different matter entirely.

So today was going to be different. Today she was going to think positively and not dwell on the past. Today she'd choose not to care.

CHAPTER SIX

GUILT WASN'T A feeling Rafael was all that familiar with, but the guilt—and shame—he felt about not going to see if Nicky was all right last night was seriously beginning to grate.

So much for assuming he'd have forgotten all about it by this morning. He'd barely thought about anything else, because he might have gone to bed convinced he'd done the best thing by leaving her alone, and he might have congratulated himself on stoically resisting the urge to give in to his instincts, but over the course of the morning the doubts that had crept in overnight had intensified and nothing was making them go away. Not the knowledge that he had at least put his ear to her door on his way to bed, not the reassuring sounds of movement coming from her room at the crack of dawn, and not the jaunty whistling he'd heard coming from the landing moments before he'd shut the back door behind him.

Not even the hard physical work he'd engaged in in the vineyards had been enough to put it from his mind because, regardless of the consequences, he *should* have paid attention to his gut and checked up on her. Quite apart from it being the gentlemanly thing to do, Nicky was a guest in his home and therefore her welfare was technically his responsibility, however much he might not want it to be.

Which really left him with only one course of action, he

thought, narrowing his eyes and glowering at the blindingly white *cortijo* he was striding towards. Never mind that it directly contravened his policy of not getting involved. Never mind that it could potentially open up a whole messy can of worms. He had no option but to ask Nicky outright what was going on, and the sooner the better because the doubts and the guilt and the shame were driving him nuts and he didn't think he could stand any of it much longer.

Pushing open the back door he strode into the hall and briefly wondered where to start hunting for her. She shouldn't be too far away. If she wasn't in the house she'd probably be—

'Rafael?'

At the sound of her voice he automatically stopped and turned. And went still as all the blood rushed to his feet and his plan to clear his conscience shot clean out of his head.

Standing in the doorway of the kitchen, Nicky wasn't too far away at all. On the contrary she was uncomfortably close, and, in a bright red bikini top, a very short turquoise skirt that sat low on her waist and nothing else, her nose a little pink from the sun and her hair still semi-wet from the pool and hanging in thick waves to her shoulders, very very appealing.

Unable to stop himself, Rafael ran his gaze over her, over the swell of her breasts, pushed up and in by the bikini top, the dip of her waist, the flat abdomen and the flaring of her hips and then down to below the hem of the itsy-bitsy skirt and those long slim legs, which he'd envisaged wrapped around his waist so often in his dreams.

She looked like some kind of siren and as lust shot through him, so hot and fast it nearly brought him to his knees, he had the feeling that if he wasn't careful, if he didn't focus on what was important here, he could well find himself being lured to his doom.

Which wasn't nearly as ominous a notion as it ought to have been. In fact as he stood there staring at her, desire pounding through him and his head whirling, doom was looking increasingly tempting, and he had to ball his hands into fists to stop himself lunging for her because he was pretty sure that that kind of behaviour would get his face slapped.

With superhuman effort Rafael swallowed hard, ruthlessly deleted all images of sultry temptresses and entwined legs from his brain, and pulled himself together because wanting her was *not* why he'd decided to seek her out. 'What?' he muttered.

'I—' She stopped and looked at him with sudden concern. 'Are you all right?'

'Absolutely fine,' he said, frustration with himself making him sound brusquer than he'd have liked. 'What about you?'

'Me?' she asked, blinking up at him in surprise. 'Oh, I couldn't be better.'

Rafael frowned. 'Are you sure?'

'Of course,' she said, and flashed him an overly bright smile. 'Why on earth wouldn't I be?'

He thought he saw her smile falter for a second, but it was back in the blink of an eye and he couldn't be certain. 'Did you sleep well?'

'Fabulously.'

'Really?'

She nodded. 'Absolutely. It must be all this fresh air and sun.'

Hmm. He tilted his head and noticed the dark shadows beneath her eyes that belied her words. 'Right.'

'You sound sceptical.'

If it hadn't been for the guilt swilling around inside him, Rafael would have let it go, but if anything the guilt was growing so instead he braced himself and made himself say, 'I am.'

'Why?'

'Because in the middle of the night I heard a yell.'

Nicky's eyebrows shot up and she froze and for a moment there was such utter silence that he could hear the hum of a tractor he knew to be miles away. 'A yell?' she said at last, way too casually to be convincing.

'That's right.'

'And you thought it was me?'

'Who else would it have been?'

She shrugged and shifted her weight from one foot to the other while her gaze slid from his and focused on a point somewhere over his left shoulder. 'I've no idea. An owl perhaps?'

An *owl*? 'It was you. What happened?'

She bit her lip, dithered for a second and then clearly decided there was no point in denying it any longer. 'I had a bad dream,' she said with a dismissive wave of her hand. 'It was nothing.'

'It didn't sound like nothing.'

The smile she gave him this time was tight. 'Look, Rafael, I appreciate your concern, really I do, but I don't want to talk about it.'

'Don't you think it might help?'

'No,' she said firmly. 'It really was nothing, and I'd be grateful if you'd drop it.'

Rafael stared at her for a second, mulling over whether he should push her further for an explanation, but then mentally shrugged and did as she asked. He'd tried, but he could hardly force her to tell him, and anyway if it really *was* nothing then he didn't need to.

In fact he ought to be relieved she didn't want to discuss it. He'd done what he'd set out to do. By bringing the matter up he'd assuaged the guilt, and Nicky's request that he leave things alone reaffirmed his judgement that she wouldn't have appreciated the interference even if he *had* rushed to her aid, so he was completely off the hook. And he hadn't even had to mop up any messy emotional stuff.

So where was the relief? Where was the satisfaction? And why was he feeling faintly piqued by her reluctance to talk about what was troubling her instead of being pleased at such a successful outcome to his quandary?

'OK, fine,' he said, nodding and deciding to attribute the baffling—and faintly disconcerting—paradox to a long morning in the sun.

'Thanks,' she said, brightening considerably and shooting him a beaming smile that had desire once again rushing through him. 'You know, you're just in time.'

To do what? Succumb to her allure and his total mental collapse? Or pick her up, toss her over his shoulder and carry her up to bed? 'For what?' he said hoarsely, and cleared his throat.

'Lunch. Or what passes for lunch in my world.' Her mouth curved up into a funny little half-smile and his stomach felt as if someone had grabbed it and twisted. Hard. 'I'm not much of a cook, I'm afraid—not enough time spent in the kitchen probably—but I've cobbled a salad together from last night's leftovers and was wondering, would you like to join me?'

No was the answer he should have been looking for if he wanted to retain any kind of sanity, but clearly he didn't because all he could think right now was that he was hungry, her smile was as inviting as the idea of food and his brain was so addled with lust, confusion and frustration on top of the lingering pangs of guilt and shame he could barely remember his own name, let alone come up with some kind of suitable excuse.

'Sure,' he said and wondered what she'd think if he walked up to the wall and started banging his head against it. 'Why not?'

'It'll be five minutes.' She tilted her head and regarded him thoughtfully. 'In the meantime, why don't you take a dip? You look a bit hot and bothered.'

Watching her saunter back into the kitchen, Rafael resisted the urge to get up close and personal with that wall, and instead shoved his hands through his hair while calling himself all kinds of idiot for being so weak.

Maybe a long morning beneath the hot sun had resulted in more than just the paradox of being piqued instead of pleased that she didn't want to talk through her issues. Maybe it was also responsible for an evident meltdown of his brain cells, because one way or another Nicky was driving him demented, as was his total inability to know what to do about any of it.

Perhaps a swim wasn't such a bad idea, he thought darkly, heading upstairs to don his swimming shorts. The icy water of the pool would no doubt have the same effect as a cold shower, and it might even clear his head long enough for him to work out how to fix the exceedingly uncomfortable problem he was still facing.

Something had to be done, because he might have sorted out one dilemma but there still remained the issue of the unrequited lust he was suffering from, which if it continued any longer could well end up doing permanent damage to his body.

The question was, what to do?

Frowning as he began to assess the options, Rafael threw a towel over his shoulder and headed back downstairs. Taking care to avoid the kitchen and the dangers that lurked within, he stepped out onto the patio and strode along the path that led to the pool, frustratingly none the wiser.

He dropped the towel on a sun lounger, walked up to the edge of the pool and dived straight in.

Perhaps he should ask Nicky to leave after all, he thought, relishing the way the icy shock that hit his body obliterated the heat inside him, and beginning to scythe through the shimmering water as he made for the other end. Maybe *he* should leave, although frankly he didn't see why he had to when it was his house.

Or maybe, just maybe, he was going about this all wrong.

Rafael reached the end and surfaced. He rubbed the water out of his eyes and drew in a deep breath as a bubble of clarity burst in his head.

God, he was, wasn't he? He was going about this in *completely* the wrong way, and frankly if he conducted his business in such a manner he'd be bankrupt within weeks. Because how could he fix this—or any problem for that matter—when he wasn't in full possession of the facts?

As was very definitely the case here. He didn't have all the facts, did he? All he knew was the way *he* was feeling, the desire and need and longing *he* was burning up with. He had no idea how Nicky felt about anything. For all he knew she could be burning up in the same way he was.

OK, so she hadn't shown any sign of it so far, but then he was pretty sure he hadn't either, so she could well be just as crazed with lust as he was and equally adept at concealing it. After all she'd been eyeing him up yesterday evening at supper, hadn't she?

And if that *was* the case then maybe she was waiting for him to make the first move. Or maybe she was as baffled by all this as he was and was also struggling to work out what to do about it.

Hmm. Whatever Nicky was or wasn't doing, and frankly his head hurt just trying to work it out, he clearly needed a new, more obvious strategy.

* * *

So much for a new and more obvious strategy, Rafael thought darkly an hour later as he fought back the urge to grind his teeth.

Honestly, short of yanking Nicky into his arms and kissing the life out of her he didn't think he could have been more obvious.

Over lunch he'd hit her with his full arsenal of moves, which admittedly wasn't huge as he'd never had to work so hard to entice a woman into his arms, but nevertheless he thought he'd done his best.

He'd complimented her on the salad that hadn't been nearly as bad as she'd made out, and had then set out to be as attentive as he could. Although she'd been remarkably unforthcoming, he'd asked her dozens of questions about herself and her work, and had happily complied when she'd turned his questions back on him. He'd been genuinely interested and he thought she'd been the same.

Encouraged by that he'd shot her endless warm smiles, flashed her wide grins he'd been told were devastating, and been as charming as he knew how. He'd even left his T-shirt and shorts off after his swim to give her ample opportunity to ogle his near-naked body should she wish to do so.

But had any of it made even the faintest scrap of difference? No, it had not. There he'd been practically combusting with lust—not least because now he didn't have to imagine what she looked like in a bikini—and Nicky couldn't have been less bothered.

To his growing frustration she'd hadn't shown the slightest interest in his body and had been spectacularly undevastated by his smiles. In fact, at one point, after a wide, and, he'd thought, particularly blinding smile, she'd frowned and had had the cheek to ask him if he was feeling all right.

Now she'd settled herself on a sun lounger, was rubbing

suncream into the legs that had been haunting his dreams, and he was slowly going insane. Unable to drag his gaze away, he had a sudden vision of those hands roaming all over him, caressing every inch of him, and his body hardened.

With desire thrumming through him Rafael picked savagely at the label of the bottle of water they'd shared over lunch.

Dammit, why didn't Nicky find him as attractive as he found her? He'd been told he was reasonably good-looking and that his body wasn't too bad. He had all his hair, which was apparently something of a rarity in men over thirty, and, apart from the edginess he'd been feeling over the last couple of days, he was generally fairly even-tempered.

So what was wrong with her?

He glowered at the label for a second and then ruthlessly cut off that train of thought because it smacked of arrogance and petulance and those were two traits he hoped he didn't possess.

He didn't expect every woman to fall at his feet; it was just that quite a few had done in the years since his divorce, so it was frustrating—not to mention hugely unflattering—when he came across one he wanted who didn't.

With a growl of frustration Rafael abandoned the bottle and lifted his glass to his mouth instead. He let a cube of ice slide between his lips, crunched down on it and winced at the sudden hit of cold.

'Would you mind doing my back?'

Rafael jerked and choked on a chunk of ice. He coughed. Pounded his chest. Swallowed hard. And then as the implication of her words hit his brain his blood roared in his ears and his heart lurched so violently he nearly passed out.

God, she really was going to kill him. Because if the mere thought of his hands on her sent him into spasms of lust what would happen when he actually touched her for real? Which he was going to have to, of course, because what else could he do?

Slathering her in warm slippery cream might well unravel what was left of his self-control but he could hardly refuse. Not when lunch had been cleared away a while ago and he was doing nothing but trying not to watch her, picking at that damned label, crunching ice and slowly going out of his mind.

Rafael dragged in a deep steadying breath and told himself to calm down. All he had to do was think of Nicky as one of his sisters, whose backs he'd rubbed cream into loads of times in the past, and it would be fine.

'Not at all,' he muttered, getting to his feet and pulling his shorts on over his trunks in the hope it might disguise his body's reaction to her. As the cotton scraped over his sensitive skin he gritted his teeth and determinedly drummed up images of icicles and igloos.

With not a little discomfort he walked over, knelt down beside her and took the bottle from her outstretched hand, and tried not to jump when their fingers brushed.

'Thanks.' Nicky beamed up at him, then settled on her front and to his horror reached behind her and unclipped her bikini top.

It was fine, he told himself again, his jaw so tight he thought it might snap. It was just a back. A long smooth one, yes, but just a back. In the same way that that was just a bottom and those were just legs.

Except that they weren't because none of her was just anything. It was all slim. Toned. Perfect.

He drew in a breath and let it out agonisingly slowly in an effort to brace himself. He could forget trying to consider Nicky a sister because it wasn't working. And he could forget the icicles and igloos because they weren't working either. He was now thinking glaciers. Ice hotels. The Arctic.

All of which melted the instant he put his hands on the silky warm skin of her shoulders. At the feel of her beneath his palms as he slid them down her back, his senses shut out everything but her. The soft texture of her skin... The dizzying scent of the lotion as he smoothed it over her. The dazzling sight of all that bare hot flesh... The muffled sounds of her sighs...

He wondered what she'd taste like and his mouth watered with such longing that his knees nearly buckled beneath the onslaught of it all. His head swam and his body burned and he couldn't help letting out a deep ragged groan.

The sound of it, so rough, so desperate, snapped him out of the sensuous whirl and brought him crashing back to reality. He jerked his hands off her, snapped back and shoved them through his hair, not caring one bit that they were still covered in cream.

God. What was he doing? What was he thinking? Had he truly lost his mind? And could he even begin to hope she hadn't heard it?

Apparently not because she tensed a little and her breath hitched. 'Rafael, are you all right?' she murmured sleepily.

'Yes,' he muttered, totally thrown by the dizzying realisation that he'd been so wholly caught up in her. 'Why?'

'You sighed. Deeply.'

'I'm fine.'

She twisted her head round, squinted up at him and frowned. 'You don't look fine. You're glowering.'

'Just thinking,' he said, and told himself he really had to get a grip before all the need, confusion, tension and frustration that were swilling around inside him snapped and he did something truly insane like flip her over, get them both naked and then sink himself inside her.

Her eyebrows shot up. 'Heavens, about what?'

'Nothing,' he said sharply and lurched to his feet. 'You're done.'

'Thank you,' she said, wriggling slightly to refasten her top. Then she sat up and stared at him. 'It doesn't look like nothing. You look like you want to rip something apart with your teeth.'

Such as that bikini? The vision of Nicky writhing beneath him as he tore the red cotton from her body slammed into his head and practically robbed him of breath. Desire clamoured even harder at the flimsy barriers he'd erected and he had the terrifying feeling that he was losing the battle to contain it any longer.

'It's work, that's all,' he said, and took a quick unsteady step back because he had to get out of here now.

'Can I do anything to help?'

Yes. Quite a few things. 'No,' he said hoarsely.

'Oh, OK.' She frowned and bit that luscious lower lip and that was the last straw really. The lust he'd been struggling to keep at bay finally crashed through the barriers and his resistance evaporated beneath the force of it.

What the hell? He thought he'd been obvious, but clearly he hadn't been nearly obvious enough. And what did he have to lose? His self-control was already in tatters. His brain was already in shreds. What would a slap to the face do that she hadn't already done to him?

'Do you *really* want to know what the problem is?' he growled, way beyond the point of no return to question the wisdom of his actions.

Nicky nodded. 'I do.'

He reached down, wrapped his hands around her arms and hauled her to her feet. '*This* is what my problem is,' he muttered, barely registering her splutter of shock as he pulled her against him.

He buried one hand in her hair, clamped the other to the

small of her back, and as she gasped crushed his mouth down on hers. He plunged his tongue between her parted lips, the desire racing along his veins, burning through his blood and setting fire to his guts. She tasted just as good as he'd imagined. Like honey. Like heaven. And she felt soft and lithe, fitting into his body as if made for him.

His head spinning with dizzying need, Rafael groaned into her mouth and pulled her even tighter against him. He angled her head and deepened the kiss, his relief at finally having her where he wanted her making him so giddy that it was some time before he realised that she wasn't responding.

But she wasn't, he realised dazedly, easing the pressure of his mouth and softening the kiss. She was just sort of… there. Hanging limply in his arms. Completely inert.

Her heart wasn't hammering like his, dammit, her body wasn't plastering itself uncontrollably against his and her breathing wasn't all ragged and shaky. She clearly wasn't being rendered boneless by the experience as he was, which meant that for the first time since confusing lust for something more and proposing to Marina he'd just made a grave error of judgement.

Rafael jerked back, let her go and as he stared down at her stunned expression it all became abundantly clear.

Nicky *didn't* feel the same way about him. She *hadn't* been waiting for him to make the first move, and she hadn't been baffled or struggling or any of the other things he'd thought she might have been doing. It had all been in his wildly overactive, desperately hopeful and seriously deluded imagination.

In other words he'd been a complete and utter fool.

CHAPTER SEVEN

OH MY GOD, thought Nicky in astonishment, touching her mouth and staring wide-eyed at Rafael as he took a step back and raked his hands through his hair.

What on earth had *that* been all about?

One minute, faintly concerned by the strangled groan he'd let out while rubbing cream into her shoulders, she'd been politely enquiring after his health, the next she'd been dragged into his arms and had the life kissed out of her.

And why would he do that? she wondered dazedly before her head cleared of the shock and the dizziness, and the only feasible answer came to her. Surely he couldn't *fancy* her, could he?

No. It was impossible. He'd shown no indication that he did. In fact, what with the whole braining him business and the way he'd kept himself so busy over the last twenty-four hours and—with the exception of supper last night—very definitely out of her way, she'd got the impression that she was more of a nuisance than an attraction. Which she could well understand because she hadn't exactly been the ideal house guest so far.

Yet there was no denying the intensity and the passion behind that kiss. She could still feel the heat of his mouth moving over hers, the pressure of his hands on her body and the tension that had vibrated through him. She could still feel his tongue sliding between her lips and tangling with hers with the kind of skill and focus that her former self would have revelled in. And she could most certainly still feel the hard length of the erection that had been throbbing so insistently against her abdomen.

Good heavens, she thought, blinking in surprise as it became pretty obvious that he did, in fact, want her. Who'd have imagined…?

If she'd given it much thought, which she hadn't, it would never have occurred to her that someone fancying her at the moment was possible. Why would anyone—especially a man like Rafael who could presumably have whichever woman he chose—when she looked like a wreck and felt about as attractive as a sack of potatoes? But as bizarre as it seemed, all the evidence suggested that was indeed the case.

So was *that* what lunch had been all about? Was that why he'd switched on the charm and shot her so many warm blinding smiles she'd had to slip on her sunglasses? Had he been *flirting* with her?

God, maybe it was and maybe he had. And like the hopeless idiot she'd become she hadn't had a clue about any of it. She'd taken his attention at face value, and, feeling so deliciously relaxed and so inordinately grateful that he'd respected her request to leave the subject of her nightmare alone, had casually returned his smiles and fielded his questions as if talking to an old friend.

Not only that but she'd asked him to rub cream into her back. She'd even taken her bikini top off, for heaven's sake. No wonder he'd flipped.

Oh, what a mess, she thought as despair and mortification flooded through her. What a horrible awkward mess. Rafael wanted her. Unfortunately she didn't want him. Where on earth did they go from here?

But before she could even begin to work out whether she

ought to offer him some sort of explanation for her lack of response, Rafael broke the excruciating tension.

'I do apologise,' he said with an icy cool formality that knocked her off balance for a second and had her suddenly wondering if maybe she'd got it all wrong. If maybe she'd imagined the scorching heat and the passion that had been pouring off him only a minute ago because there was absolutely none of *that* left, was there? Nor was there any sign of the raw, out-of-control desperation she'd sensed in him when he'd been kissing her. In fact the man standing in front of her with the blank expression on his face, the shutters down over his eyes and the air of tight self-control surrounding him was almost unrecognisable, and to be honest she found the abrupt switch perplexing and not a little disconcerting.

'Whatever for?' she said, dragging herself back to what he'd said and thinking that if anyone had to apologise, surely it was her.

'Assaulting you,' he said flatly. 'It was unforgivable. I'm sorry.'

What? 'Assaulting me?' she echoed her eyebrows lifting as the feeling of having stepped into an alternate reality grew. 'You didn't assault me. You kissed me. There's a difference.'

'Is there?' The flatness of his voice suggested he didn't agree.

'Of course.'

He shoved his hands in the pockets of his shorts and his jaw tightened. 'You didn't respond.'

And that made him think he'd assaulted her? Hmm, however unpalatable an in-depth explanation for her lack of response might be, she couldn't let him think that. 'Well, no,' Nicky admitted, 'but that wasn't your fault.'

'Wasn't it?'

'No.' She shook her head vehemently and gave him a

faint smile. 'I mean, let's face it, you're gorgeous and most women would have swooned at that kiss.'

'But not you.'

Her smile faded. 'No. But really, it's not you. It's me.'

She didn't think it would be possible but Rafael went even stiller and his jaw tightened even more and she inwardly cringed because it might be true but it was still one of the most hackneyed lines on the planet. 'It really *is* me,' she added, but that didn't sound any better.

'Forget it,' he said with a dismissive shrug.

'I can't,' she said, 'because you have no idea how much I *want* to find you attractive.' He winced and she sighed in despair because instead of making things better she was only making them worse. 'If you'd just let me explain...'

'You don't have to explain anything.'

'I do.'

'There's really no need.'

'I think there is.'

And then his stonily blank mask slipped for a second, his eyes suddenly flashing as he glowered at her. 'Look, Nicky,' he snapped and she jumped. 'For the briefest of moments I found you attractive. Maybe it was the heat. The wine. Or the sun. Whatever. It was an error of judgement on my part, a mistake and an aberration. I apologise for it and you can be sure it won't happen again, but it really doesn't warrant discussion.'

'Yes, it does—' she began, but broke off when he whipped up his hand to put a halt to whatever she'd been about to say.

'No. This morning you asked me to leave the subject of your nightmare alone. Now I'm asking you to return the courtesy. So please. Just leave it.'

'But—'

'Now.'

At the hard, unyielding tone of his voice Nicky fell silent.

She looked at him for a long few seconds and then gave up. What was the point of trying to force an explanation and an apology onto him when he was in such an unreceptive frame of mind? There'd be plenty of time for that later anyway, once they'd both had a chance to cool down and reflect. Although frankly, if Rafael got any cooler he'd qualify for cryogenic preservation.

'OK. Fine,' she said grudgingly. 'I'll drop it.' *For now.*

'Good,' he said curtly and swiped up his T-shirt. 'Now please excuse me. There are things I need to see to.'

The distant sound of her mobile ringing in the kitchen filtered through the haze of her sleep-filled siesta, and Nicky yawned and stretched. She got up and padded down the stairs, her head beginning to spin yet again with the strange turn of events that the afternoon had taken.

So much for attempting to explain her behaviour, for trying to apologise. She'd done her level best, she really had, but for some reason Rafael had thwarted her every attempt.

In fact she probably shouldn't have bothered to try in the first place, she thought as she headed in the direction of the increasingly loud ringing, because hadn't he told her that he steered well clear of emotional mess? He had, so presumably the last thing he was hankering after was a spilling out of her soul, and in that they were in perfect agreement. Actually, apart from Gaby, it was about the only thing she and Rafael *did* have in common.

And as they were never going be anything more than the merest of acquaintances she really didn't need to waste any more time worrying about it. She had no need to ponder the odd way he'd gone from scorchingly hot to icily cold by the pool. No need to question the steely indifference he'd chosen to adopt, and no need to try to work out what was going on in his head any more than he needed to try and work out what was going on in hers.

No, she needed to pour all her energy to recovery. Recovery and staying well out of his way.

Spying her phone vibrating on the huge scrubbed pine table that sat in the centre of the kitchen, Nicky walked over, picked it up and hit the little green button. 'Hello?'

'Nicky!' came the relieved shriek down the phone, and at the sound of Gaby's voice she pushed all thoughts of perplexing men to one side and felt herself smile.

'Well, hello, stranger,' she said, pulling out a chair and sitting down.

'God, I'm sorry. I lost my phone and all the numbers and *everything* and it's taken an age to get a new one.'

'So that's why I couldn't get hold of you.'

'No one's been able to. It's been a *total* pain.' As Gaby's entire life was contained in her phone, Nicky could imagine her distress.

'How's Bahrain?'

'Hot. And depressingly dry, in all senses of the word. But more importantly, how are you?'

Hmm. Now wasn't that the question of the century? Quite honestly, what with everything that had been going on lately Nicky wasn't sure she knew any more. 'Fine,' she said in the absence of having any idea what else to say.

'Really?'

'Well, getting there,' she amended as it suddenly struck her that maybe she was. Maybe the *cortijo had* begun to work its magic, because, now she thought about it, of all the emotions that had been churning through her in the last couple of days—and there'd been plenty—despair and desolation had been conspicuous by their absence.

'Good. And how are your chakras?'

She thought about it a bit more and felt surprisingly light, as if the dark heavy weight she'd been carrying around for so long was beginning to lift a little. And then her smile deepened as the light at the end of that tunnel glowed a fraction brighter. 'Beginning to align, it would seem.'

'Hah,' said Gaby triumphantly. 'I knew it. God, I'm good.'

Nicky sat back in the chair, lifted her knees and planted her heels on the edge of the seat. 'Not that good,' she said dryly, wrapping her arm around her ankles and hugging her knees to her chest. 'I thought you swore your brother never came down here.'

'He doesn't. Or at least he hasn't for ages.'

'He does now.'

There was long, rather stunned silence. 'Rafa's there?'

'Yes.' At least she imagined he was. Probably seeing to those 'things' that had suddenly demanded such urgent attention.

'Good Lord. Why?'

Nicky paused and racked her brains because she could hardly tell Gaby her brother had been escaping his sisters. 'I think he was after a bit of rest and relaxation,' she said vaguely.

Gaby blew out a breath. 'Oh, I *am* sorry.'

'Why? It's not your fault.'

'No, I guess not. I mean, I did try and contact him, but he wouldn't answer any of my calls and he didn't reply to any of my emails…It never occurred to me he'd actually show up, though.'

'Well, he did,' Nicky muttered, catching sight of a slip of paper propped up against the vase of flowers sitting in the centre of the table. She leaned forwards to read the short note and then sat back and frowned, not at all sure what to make of it. 'But now it seems he's gone.'

There was a pause. 'Gone? Gone where?

'Back to Madrid.'

'Why?'

An excellent question. 'Work, according to the note I've just found.'

There was a moment's silence while Gaby processed the information. 'That doesn't make any sense at all.'

'Well, it is Sunday,' said Nicky, propping the piece of paper back where she'd found it. 'So I guess he had to get back for Monday.'

'But it's August,' said Gaby, sounding utterly baffled. 'No one works in August.'

Nicky bit her lip and tried to ignore the niggling suspicion that he'd planned to stay longer than just the weekend and had it not been for her he'd still be there. 'Apart from Rafael apparently,' she said, and then added as much to reassure herself as Gaby, 'You said yourself that he's a workaholic.'

Gaby sighed. 'That's true, I suppose. What else did his note say?'

'Not a lot. Just that I'm to enjoy the rest of my holiday.'

'I second that… So tell me everything. How did Rafael take you being there?'

Nicky grimaced as snapshots of the last couple of days flashed through her memory. 'I don't think he was entirely happy about it.' Which had to be the understatement of the century.

'No, well, he only has himself to blame,' said Gaby huffily. 'If he'd bothered to get in touch I could have explained everything.'

'It was fine,' said Nicky and hoped she wouldn't be struck down for the little white lie. 'Rafael spent most of the time talking to his vines and I've spent most of it reading by the pool. And that's—er—about it.'

Gaby hmmed sceptically. 'Now why do I get the feeling you're not telling me everything?'

Probably because Nicky sounded as guilty as hell, even

though she didn't really have anything to be guilty about. But heavens, now really wasn't a good time for Gaby to have one of her flashes of insight, because she was, after all, Rafael's sister, and, while Nicky didn't have any siblings so she didn't know for sure, she doubted Gaby would feel comfortable knowing exactly what had gone on by the pool any more than *she* would be discussing it.

'Nicky?'

She stifled a sigh and ran a hand through her hair. 'I can't imagine,' she said and cringed because it would have been hard to sound less convincing.

'Could it be because you're being uncharacteristically evasive?'

Nicky could virtually see her friend's antennae quivering, and pinched the bridge of her nose. 'I'm not being evasive,' she said. Evasively.

Gaby sucked in a breath and then said in a steely voice that Nicky had never heard before, 'What did he do?'

Nicky felt herself go bright red and thanked God Gaby wasn't around to see it. 'Nothing.'

'Rubbish. I know my brother. Did he make a pass at you or something?'

She wriggled in her chair and thought that however uncomfortable it made either of them, she'd have to come clean because one thing she'd discovered about her neighbour was that she might be all about balance and peace and chakras but she could be ruthlessly relentless in her pursuit of the truth when the mood took her.

'It was just a kiss,' she said lightly. 'That's all. Rafael kissed me, we had a—ah—little chat about it, and then at some point between then and now he must have gone.'

Long seconds of silence ticked by. So many of them, in fact, that Nicky wondered if they'd been cut off. 'Gaby? Are you still there?'

'I'm here.'

'Did you hear what I said?'

'I did.'

'And are you reassured?'

There was a pause and then it was as if Gaby sort of exploded. 'Reassured? *Reassured?* Are you joking? I'm not reassured in the least. In fact I'm going to kill him,' she spluttered. 'I'm going to bloody kill him.'

Rafael slammed closed the door to his flat, dumped his things in the hall and headed straight to the fridge for a cool refreshing beer. Flipping off the lid, he lifted the bottle to his mouth, leaned back against the counter and took a long swallow.

God, what an afternoon.

As the harrowing memory of it slammed back into his head for the thousandth time since he'd packed up and left he closed his eyes and let out a long deep breath.

How could he have got it all so badly wrong? How could he have so totally lost control like that? How could his rock-solid resistance to temptation have vaporised quite so comprehensively?

His behaviour had been unfamiliar, unexpected and completely unprecedented. And as for the primal urge to stake some sort of claim on Nicky, the one that had surged through him and had made him reach down and grab her, well, that had simply been as scary as hell.

At least in the aftermath of the kiss he'd managed to wrestle back *some* degree of control, he thought with a shudder. At least he hadn't high-tailed it to the safety of his vines as he'd been so tempted to do, but instead had stayed there, strong and resolute and in control. And at least he hadn't revealed any of the turmoil and confusion and still-scorching desire that had been churning through him. That really would have finished him off.

Yes, cool indifference and a refusal to let her speak had been the right way to handle it because he'd had no intention of engaging in a discussion about what had happened and he certainly hadn't wanted her to rake over the way he'd behaved or analyse his many deficiencies.

Leaving had been a good idea too because, for one thing, Nicky might have agreed to back off but the look in her eye had been fiercely determined and he'd got the impression she was planning to revisit the discussion at the first available opportunity.

For another, he might not have wanted to admit it, but her rejection of him had hurt and he didn't really need to be constantly reminded of it every time he laid eyes on her.

And lastly, with his self-control in such bits he couldn't guarantee that kissing her wouldn't happen again, and if that wasn't the most terrifying thought on the planet he didn't know what was.

So he'd walked away from her with what little pride he'd had left, utterly exhausted and defeated and struck by the realisation that finally, *finally* he'd reached breaking point.

Rafael sighed and rubbed a hand over his face. It had truly been the most shattering, frustrating, painful weekend he'd had in years and frankly he couldn't wait to see the back of it.

At least it was nearly over, he told himself, glancing up at the clock. He'd use what was left of it and the rest of the beer in the fridge to wipe it from his head, and put Nicky out of his mind once and for all. Then all the stuff churning around inside him would settle down, things would get better and he'd start to feel normal again.

With any luck.

The sound of his phone ringing jerked Rafael out of his thoughts. He dug it out of his pocket and as he glanced at the screen he inwardly groaned because apparently things weren't going to get better just yet.

Resisting the temptation to ignore the call because look at what had happened the last time he'd done that, he hit the answer button and lifted the phone to his ear.

'Gaby,' he said, and took another swig from the bottle. 'Good of you to get in touch. How's Bahrain?'

'Don't you give me any of that good-of-you-to-get-in-touch-how's-Bahrain crap,' said his sister, sounding so uncharacteristically fierce that he tensed, every one of his instincts instantly jumping to high alert. 'What I want to know is, what the hell did you do to my friend?'

Carefully setting down his beer, Rafael forced himself to relax and stay cool. 'I take it you've spoken to Nicky.'

'I've just got off the phone to her.'

'How is she?'

Gaby blew out a furious breath. 'Oh, she's fine. Just fine, considering… Me, though, I'm in a state of shock.'

He closed his eyes for a second and ignored the urge to hang up and blame it on a low battery. 'Why? What did she say?'

'That you'd kissed her.'

'I see.'

Gaby spluttered a bit more. 'Is that it?'

Rafael stifled a sigh. 'What else do you want me to say? You seem to know everything already.'

'Not everything,' she said furiously. 'One thing I'd really like to know is, how *could* you?'

Pretty easily, he thought, as the memory of Nicky in his arms and how she'd got there flashed in his head. Stamping down on the sudden surge of desire that rushed through him, he forced himself to focus on the conversation.

'What's your problem, Gaby? Why the outrage?'

In contrast to him Nicky hadn't seemed particularly upset

by the kiss earlier so what was his sister so het up about? Had Nicky had time to reflect and reached the same conclusion that he had? Had she decided that he had in fact taken one hell of a liberty, and said as much to Gaby? 'It was only a kiss,' he muttered as a sense of unease and a ribbon of self-disgust wound through him.

'That's precisely the problem,' his sister said vehemently. 'Nicky does *not* need kissing. She's in enough of a mess as it is without you adding to it.'

Rafael frowned. 'What kind of mess?'

'It's not for me to say.'

'Gaby...'

'No. She asked me not to. But it's serious.'

A chill ran through him. 'Is she ill?'

'No. At least not physically, I don't think. But what I *will* say is that she's been going through a really rough time lately and could do with a bit of head-space. She needs a break and time to get herself back together. Alone.'

And just like that, as if he didn't have enough to contend with, a bucketload of guilt landed on top of all the frustration and desire and self-recrimination, and his head began to pound with the force of it.

God, he should have realised something wasn't quite right with Nicky. In fact, he had, hadn't he? Within five minutes of meeting her he'd noticed the paleness of her face and the fact that she was a little too thin. He'd seen the way she'd tensed up when they'd talked about her work yesterday evening at supper, and he'd registered the way she'd been so reticent to talk about herself today at lunch. And then what about that nightmare she'd had, and he'd conveniently let drop?

Yes, all the signs that she wasn't entirely OK had been there. And what had he done? He'd paid it all the barest attention and then like a self-centred jerk switched his focus to himself, completely consumed by the heat and desire she'd

aroused in him and outraged by the fact that it wasn't re-
ciprocated.

And then he'd jumped on her.

As yet more self-disgust unfurled in the pit of his stomach
and spread throughout his body Rafael wished he'd never
made the decision to head south. He wished he'd stayed
right here and suffered whatever torture that dinner party
might have held, whatever lengths Elisa might have gone
to to make him change his mind, because frankly none of
it would have been as unpalatable as having to live with the
knowledge that his behaviour over the last forty-eight hours
was nothing to be proud of.

'Well, I'm back at home,' he said flatly, 'and as I have no
intention of laying eyes on her ever again, Nicky can have
all the head-space she needs.'

CHAPTER EIGHT

MUCH TO HER surprise, Nicky was enjoying the rest of her so-called holiday immensely. Whether it was because the *cortijo* was so quiet and tranquil it was impossible not to relax, or whether it was because Rafael was no longer around to bamboozle her poor frazzled brain, she had no idea. All she knew was that in the fortnight since he'd left, she'd settled into something of a routine that largely revolved around eating, sleeping, reading and sunbathing, and she was feeling better than she had in ages.

The Monday following his stealthy departure Maria had returned after her weekend off and had resumed her mission to feed Nicky up. A seemingly never-ending stream of dishes had appeared, each so mouth-wateringly appetising that Nicky couldn't have resisted even if she'd wanted to. Slivers of melt-in-the-mouth *jamón*. Little earthenware pots of sizzling hot green peppers. Bowls of steaming paella. Strong crumbly manchego cheese. Spicy chorizo, sun-warmed tomatoes picked straight from the vines and freshly baked bread… She devoured it all and as a result had put on a few pounds, which she reckoned suited her.

Filled with good food, she'd been sleeping a lot better. Once she'd got used to the creaks and groans of the two-hundred-year-old house, she found the silence of the night comforting, and tended to crash out the minute her head hit the pillow. Not stirring until dawn, she enjoyed a sleep that was deep and restorative and nightmare-free.

Well, *almost* nightmare-free. She'd had it again once a week ago, triggered, she suspected, by a phone call from her therapist who was ringing to see how she was, but that was it. Most nights she seemed to dream of Rafael, which was bizarre given that he barely crossed her mind during the day.

Feeling physically so much stronger, Nicky had taken to exploring. The minute she opened the shutters to the coral pink streaks slashing across the sky, she was up, showered and dressed and heading outside into the relative cool of an Andalucian August morning.

As the sun inched higher she wandered up and down the rows of vines, letting the heady scent of ripening grapes and dry, dusty earth envelop her and feeling the warmth of the soil beneath her flip-flops stealing right into the depths of her bones and absorbing the cold that had been there for so long.

She'd got into the habit of having a nap after lunch, then spent the afternoons swimming and reading. In the evenings she sat on the terrace, looked out over the gently rolling landscape, nibbled on tapas and drank wine, the warm night air vibrating with the chirrup of cicadas and redolent with the scent of mosquito-busting citronella.

Not only had she been sleeping—and looking better—but she'd also tentatively been getting back in touch with friends and colleagues. Yesterday she'd even emailed her parents to find out where they were and how they were getting on.

Best of all, this morning she'd woken up, seen the fabulous light that she saw every morning, and without even thinking about it had picked up her camera. Her body buzzing with anticipation and her heart racing, she'd gone outside into the vines as usual, but, instead of idly ambling through them and thinking about nothing, this time she'd found herself automatically studying the way the light fell on the fat ripe grapes and bounced off the browning crumbling leaves, and focusing on contrast, angles and composition.

She'd rattled off a series of pictures and before she'd known it the sun was high in the sky and she was sweltering and dirty and aching all over. And she'd never felt so good, so giddy with delight, so *relieved*.

All she had to do now, she thought, pulling her eye mask down and settling against the pillows for her customary siesta, was wait for her libido to come back and she'd be well and truly on the road to recovery.

There was someone in the house.

Jolted out of the deep sleep she'd been enjoying, Nicky sat bolt upright in bed and tore off her eye mask, her pulse hammering, her blood roaring in her ears, and every one of her instincts quivering with awareness.

The slam of the front door echoed off the walls and the heavy thud of footsteps pounding up the stairs resounded through the house, shaking the *cortijo*'s foundations and rattling the windows.

Her ears pricked. Each step seemed to hit the floor in time to her heartbeat, getting closer, louder, faster as they thumped along the corridor, making straight for her room. Her stomach churned and she went dizzy.

It was just like before, she thought, her breath catching. Only this time it was the middle of the day. This time she wasn't white-knuckled and terrified. This time she wasn't frantically hunting around for a weapon and trembling with panic. And yes, her heart was pounding, but it wasn't with fear; it was with something else entirely because those footsteps sounded familiar. Very familiar. And even though they'd been gone a while now they were, apparently, back.

Before she could even begin to try and work out why, her

door flung back and there was Rafael, standing in the space where it had once been, looking haggard and drained, but dark and intense and utterly gorgeous nonetheless.

For one agonisingly long moment neither of them spoke. On Nicky's part, her head had gone so blank that all she could do was stare at him. And as for Rafael, she somehow got the impression that he didn't trust himself to speak. He looked to be barely clinging onto his control, as if it were taking every ounce of his strength to stay where he was. He looked like a man at the end of his tether. Like a man on the edge, and the rush of heat that swept through her made her entire body shudder and a thousand shivery little thrills scuttle up and down her spine.

Her eyes locked with his, held, and her heart skipped a beat at the fire that blazed in their depths.

'What are you doing back here?' she said, her mind spinning because no reason she could think of for his return seemed likely.

'I couldn't stay away,' he said hoarsely, his jaw tight as he stared back at her. 'I tried. But I couldn't.'

Nicky swallowed to work some moisture into her desert-dry mouth. 'Oh,' she breathed. 'Why not?'

'I can't get you out of my mind,' he said raggedly. 'You're driving me crazy.'

'What do you want me to do about it?' she said, her voice sounding oddly husky while her heart pounded so madly she thought it might break free.

And then the taut mask of his expression collapsed and the raw naked desire that was revealed nearly made her swoon. 'Put me out of my misery.'

The sizzle in the pit of her stomach flared into life and exploded, rushing through her veins like a tidal wave, drowning out all rational thought and dissolving her bones.

Somehow managing to get to her feet, Nicky slowly

walked over to him, and smiled as she took his hand and drew him towards her. She took a step back, he took one forwards and like that they tangoed towards the bed she'd just slid out of, their gazes bound by an invisible thread of want, barely touching, yet generating so much electricity that she could feel the air vibrate with it.

The backs of her knees hit the edge of the mattress, but he didn't stop and as he came up against her and took her in his arms she wound her arms around his neck and lifted her head. He lowered his and their mouths met. Opened. Fused.

She closed her eyes and sank into him and what had started as a slow, seductive meeting of mouths deepened, grew more passionate, more frenzied.

Electrifying desire shot through her and, unable to stop herself, she pressed herself closer and moaned into his mouth. Lost in a whirlpool of sensation, she felt him ease her back and down onto the bed and then clothing disintegrated and his hands were everywhere, sliding over her burning skin and touching and exploring every inch of her, her neck, her breasts, her stomach and then the molten, aching centre of her.

His mouth followed, creating devastation wherever it roamed, and within minutes she was moaning his name, writhing and panting and tilting her hips, her insides winding into an impossibly tight knot.

As wave after wave of sensation cascaded over her, Nicky groaned. Whimpered. Whispered in his ear and raked her nails across his back as she told him what she wanted.

And then he was above her and pushing inside her. Moving slowly at first but soon, with her pleas for more filling the room, driving in and out of her faster and harder, making her whole body tighten and tremble until she couldn't bear the pleasure any longer and—

Nicky woke with a start, her heart pounding, her breathing ragged, her skin coated in sweat and her insides adrift.

Oh, dear God. What was *that*?

She whipped her eye mask off, winced at the sudden flood of bright light that hit her eyes and then rapidly blinked. Which might have helped her eyes adjust, but did nothing to clear her head of the erotic images swimming around it, nor anything to dispel the tingles of residual pleasure that were rippling through her body and telling her that it could well have been what she thought it was.

Groggily levering herself up, she sat there stunned for a moment or two, then, taking a couple of deep breaths to try and clear her head and calm down, she braced herself and looked down at her T-shirt-and-knicker-clad body. Down to where the skin of her chest was flushed, her nipples were rock hard and her stomach and her legs were still twitching.

Heavens, she thought in astonishment, pressing her palms to her cheeks and feeling them burn even more fiercely at the dawning realisation that there was no longer any doubt that it had been *exactly* what she thought it was.

Well, well, well…

She flopped back and felt a wide smile spread across her face as she stretched and revelled in the unfamiliar lethargy of her body. Details of what she and Rafael had done in her sleep flitted through her head, in vivid Technicolor and spectacular clarity, and her smile deepened as heat flooded through her all over again.

Oh, thank *God*. It looked as though her much-missed sex drive was back. And about time too because she'd been beginning to fear it might *never* happen. Despite her secret efforts to encourage it…

The way her libido had reappeared might have been somewhat startling but that her dream had featured Rafael didn't surprise her in the slightest. When he'd initially gone she'd pretty much completely cast him from her mind, but at some point over the last fortnight he'd started to invade her thoughts with increasing frequency.

She'd found herself recalling the heavy weight of him lying on top of her flat out on the floor, that first night. Or remembering how well his T-shirt had stretched across the muscles of his back when he'd been lighting the barbecue and preparing the steaks.

In her mind's eye she'd kept seeing his long brown fingers twirling the stem of his wine glass and the heat in his eyes when he'd watched her eat all those prawns. And she'd kept thinking about all those smouldering sexy smiles he'd given her the next day at lunch and the feel of his hands massaging suntan lotion into her back.

And then, of course, there was that kiss by the pool.

She'd been dwelling on that a *lot*… The need in his eyes as they'd blazed down into hers. His warmth as it wrapped around her. The hard, lean planes of his body. His large hands holding her, pressing her against all that muscle and strength. That mouth, moving over hers with such skill and determination, and then the hard length of his erection pressing against her. Even the icy aloofness with which he'd dealt with the aftermath of it had been sexy in a perverse kind of way.

Not wanting to jinx things, she'd put the tingles that had run through her whenever she'd thought about him down to too much sun, but there was little point in denying it now.

She wanted him. She *wanted* him. Right now, at the mere *thought* of him, her body was weakening and softening. She just had to conjure up one of those devastating smiles and— ah, yes—her pulse was racing and her bones were melting and her temperature was rocketing in a way that had nothing to do with the midday heat.

And if she could feel all this just by thinking about him,

imagine what would happen when she and Rafael finally got together...

Nicky shivered. They'd be explosive. Dynamite. Fabulous.

If they got together, she amended, frowning suddenly and feeling the heat and desire ebb a little. Because it was all very well discovering that her libido was back and she wanted him quite desperately, but getting together would be pretty tricky when she was here and he was in Madrid, wouldn't it?

Not to mention the fact that it was entirely possible he wouldn't be interested in getting together anyway. Yes, he might have wanted her for that nanosecond he'd kissed her, but the way he'd gone so cool and indifferent minutes afterwards—although spine-tinglingly sexy—was hardly the sign of someone craving more, was it? Nor was the way he'd then vanished.

For a second her stomach plummeted, and then she jack-knifed up, pulled her shoulders back and stiffened her spine.

No, she thought, determination swooping down to fill every corner of her body and obliterating the remnants of her orgasm. After everything she'd been through she was damned if she was going to let this opportunity slip by just because of five hundred miles and a trickle of doubt.

She had to at least *see* if Rafael might be up for turning her dream into a reality because frankly, what with the excellent progress she'd made so far, she'd never forgive herself if she didn't.

CHAPTER NINE

Where he'd gone wrong last time, thought Rafael, sitting at the desk in his study in his penthouse and twirling a pen between his fingers, was in believing that he could ignore someone whose presence was so tangible even when she physically wasn't.

That was why he hadn't been able to get Nicky out of his head the weekend he'd been at the *cortijo*, he realised now, despite spending such relatively little time in her company. That was why she'd occupied his thoughts while he'd been out there in the fields, why she'd invaded his dreams, and why he'd imagined he could smell her scent even though she'd been nowhere to be seen. It was never easy to ignore a guest, however out of sight, and he'd been nuts to assume that it would be.

Distance was what he'd needed in order to wipe Nicky and the temporary but devastating havoc she'd wreaked on his well-ordered life from his mind. Distance and time. Both of which he'd had plenty of lately.

The two weeks he'd been back in Madrid had been exactly what was required to restore calm to his life, harness his self-control and rebuild the defences she'd so swiftly and comprehensively destroyed. And just what he'd needed to finally relax.

With pretty much the whole of the country shutting down

in August and almost every Madrileño beetling off to the coast or the countryside, Rafael had figured the solitude would suit him perfectly, and had stayed put.

He could easily hang out here, he'd told himself. His flat was at the top of one of the most luxurious buildings in Madrid, and had all the trappings one would expect from a penthouse, so it hadn't exactly been a hardship.

He'd spent hours poring over his beloved first edition of John Gerard's *The Herball or Generall Historie of Plantes*, and pottering around his extensive and plant-stuffed roof terrace. He'd ploughed up and down the building's lavish outdoor pool and had frequented the gym. He'd been out a couple of times with the few friends who had stayed in the city, and in between all that he'd started to research his next job.

From Nicky he thankfully hadn't heard a word. Nor had he heard from any of the other women who'd been so hell-bent on upsetting his existence. Apart from a text from Elisa informing him that she was on the Costa Brava should he feel like joining her—which he didn't—she too had been mercifully quiet. Even his family appeared to have better things to do than hassle him, and had left him alone.

Which all bode extremely well for the long sabbatical from women he'd decided to take in the wake of everything that had happened recently.

He glowered at his laptop and his mood darkened as he reminded himself exactly how dangerous Nicky, in particular, was. The others might be thorns in his side, but she was the one who turned him into someone he didn't recognise and didn't want to be. Someone who'd unravelled so quickly and comprehensively that he hadn't given even the most fleeting consideration to the values with which he conducted his relationships.

Because not only wasn't she too well—as his sister had

so brutally informed him—but Nicky was also a friend of Gaby's, and how that fact had managed to elude him at the time he had no idea.

Rafael's blood chilled as he thought about the far too close a shave he'd had. OK, so at some point during that weekend he'd evidently lost his mind, but how on earth could he have so *totally* forgotten his vow to not get involved with any friend of his sisters? It truly beggared belief.

Hadn't he learned the hard way that down that route lay disaster? Hadn't his brief, disastrous marriage proved it? And hadn't he sworn that he'd never let it happen again? He'd nearly lost one sister over the whole sorry episode and he had no intention of losing another. Ever.

Rafael had never imagined being *pleased* to have been rejected, but time and time again over the last fortnight he'd thanked God Nicky hadn't been interested in him, because if she had, and things had gone beyond one brief kiss, who knew what kind of chaos that might have caused?

But it was fine, he thought, letting out a long slow breath of relief. He'd escaped. Narrowly, but who cared? Narrowly was good enough.

Whatever had been going on in his head that weekend, and frankly it made him shudder to think about it, it was over. It had been a blip. A one-off moment of weakness, and ultimately entirely forgettable.

As was Nicky.

Now she was actually here Nicky wasn't at all sure that she'd done the right thing by coming. Yesterday afternoon, when, filled with delight and relief that she was more or less back to her old self, she'd made a plan that involved jumping on a train bound for Madrid this morning, it had felt like the most sensible, the most *right* decision she'd ever taken.

But now she was standing at Rafael's front door, her finger poised at the bell, and all the bubbling self-confidence and heart-pounding adrenalin were draining away leaving nothing but an unfamiliar bundle of nerves twisting her stomach.

Because what if he wasn't in? What if, despite Gaby's claim to the contrary, he was away at the coast as everyone else seemed to be? What if her mad dash to Madrid hadn't been the best decision she'd ever made but stupidly and uncharacteristically reckless and completely in vain?

Oh, this was ridiculous, she thought, frowning at a knot in the wood of the front door and giving herself a mental slap. She'd gone to great lengths to get here, starting with wangling Rafael's address out of Gaby on the very flimsy pretext of needing to forward some post, then facing the daunting prospect of a crowded station, and she was not going to give up this opportunity to find out whether her disturbingly long period of sexual abstinence could be at an end.

She'd had enough of being a wimp at the mercy of her hangups, and, besides, what was the worst that could happen? That he didn't answer? Or that he did, and slammed the door in her face?

Telling herself that she'd cross those bridges if and when she came to them Nicky took a deep breath, pressed the bell and waited.

As the seconds ticked by with agonising slowness she ran a hand through her hair and nibbled on her lip. Shifted her weight from one foot to the other and fiddled unnecessarily with the zip of her handbag until the jitteriness bouncing inside her got so bad her knees started trembling.

Honestly, what *was* the matter with her? She never used to get this nervous, so why now? Briefly closing her eyes and telling herself to calm down, she took a series of deep measured breaths until her pulse slowed and the pressure inside her eased.

Just in time, she thought, hearing the sound of footsteps approaching on the other side of the door and feeling a flood of relief wash over her at the realisation that at least *some-one* was home and her journey hadn't been entirely in vain.

Nicky opened her eyes as whoever it was—and she fervently hoped it was Rafael—stopped at the door, and, during the pause in which he presumably checked her out through the spyhole, she fixed her sunniest smile to her face and gave him a little wave.

Neither of which he appeared to appreciate, judging by the brief but heartfelt burst of Spanish that hit the door. She winced and dropped her hand to her side, and then jumped at the thud that sounded like either a fist or a head being thumped against the door.

Oh, dear. That didn't sound too promising, did it? In fact that sounded as if he wasn't pleased to see her at all. But that was fine. She had a plan, and she wasn't about to back out of it just because he might not be cooperative. In fact she couldn't wait to put it into action.

If only he'd open the damned door and let her in.

As the seconds continued to roll by and she found herself *still* face to face with a great flat lump of solid oak, Nicky was contemplating cupping her hands to the door and demanding he let her in when there came a muffled sigh, the latch clicked, the door swung open and there he was, towering over her, tall and broad, his face and his eyes utterly inscrutable.

But, at that particular moment, whether or not Rafael was pleased to see her didn't seem to matter, because as she looked up into his face and then straight into his eyes a great thump of desire thwacked her right in the stomach and nearly wiped out her knees.

The memory of him kissing her, his big, hard body wrapped around hers, flew into her head, making her pulse race and her breathing go haywire. As he thrust one hand into the pocket of his shorts she glanced at the other one resting on the door frame and had a sudden vision of his hands running over her sun-warmed skin. Heat wound through her and pooled in the pit of her stomach and she went dizzy.

God, if she'd needed any confirmation that her sex drive was back she had it. It was back with such a vengeance it was kind of mind-blowing to think that at one point she hadn't been interested in him at all.

Taking a deep breath before she started hyperventilating and melted into a puddle of lust, Nicky blinked to dispel the images and swallowed hard. 'Hi,' she said a lot more breathily than she'd have liked.

'Nicky,' he said flatly.

'Rafael,' she said, choosing to ignore the distinct lack of enthusiasm in his voice and giving him a beaming smile. 'How are you?'

'Fine.'

'Can I come in?'

He frowned. Hesitated for a moment, and she had the sudden disconcerting feeling he was going to slam the door in her face. But then the frown disappeared, that oddly sexy aloofness returned and as he held it back instead her stomach settled. 'Of course.'

'Thank you.'

She stepped inside, taking great care to fleetingly and subtly brush against him, and felt a dizzying little dart of satisfaction when he flinched. Excellent. Rafael might be trying to project an air of studied indifference and supreme self-control, but chemistry didn't seem to be going along with it any more than she was. Which was lucky because her plans for the afternoon relied heavily on chemistry.

'How did you know where to find me?' he said, closing the door behind her and sounding as if he wished she hadn't.

'Gaby gave me your address.'

'I didn't hear the buzzer.'

'I didn't ring it.'

'So who let you in?'

'A fellow resident.' She didn't see any need to mention that, not at all sure he'd want to see her, she'd abandoned the buzzer in favour of hovering outside, waiting for someone to go into the building and slipping in behind them. 'From downstairs, apparently. He was charming.'

'I'm sure he was.'

'He spoke flawless English.'

'How convenient.'

'Wasn't it?'

Rafael folded his arms over his chest, leaned back against the console table and fixed her with that unwavering stare that before had made her squirm with discomfort and now made her squirm with something else entirely. 'So how have you been?'

'Fabulous,' she said as longing spread through her veins as slow and thick and delicious as treacle.

Languidly and thoroughly he ran his gaze over her, from the hair on her head right down to her pink toenails, and as she endured his scrutiny every inch of her in between burned. By the time he'd finished making his way back up she was shaking inside with the effort of not hurling herself at him.

'You certainly look fab—' He broke off. Frowned. Swore probably, she thought, beneath his breath. 'Well,' he finished.

'Thank you,' she said and reminded herself that there'd be no hurling of anyone anywhere yet because she needed to concentrate. 'I feel well.'

'Would you like a drink?' he said, pushing himself off the console table and striding off in the direction of the kitchen.

'Anything soft and cold would be great,' she said and followed him despite the lack of invitation. 'It's hot, isn't it?'

He walked over to the fridge and took out a jug of orange juice and she took the opportunity to ogle his bottom. 'Very,' he muttered, and she got the delightful feeling he wasn't just referring to the temperature.

As Rafael plucked a couple of glasses from the cupboard next to the fridge and poured the juice Nicky watched the muscles of his back twist beneath the cotton of his T-shirt and her palms itched with the need to touch him.

He turned abruptly and handed her a glass.

'Thank you,' she said, taking it, lifting it to her mouth and taking a long swallow. Skin-pricklingly aware that his eyes were on her, she ran her hand down her throat as she did so. 'Yum, delicious.'

Rafael didn't move but she thought she caught the tell-tale hammering of a muscle in his jaw, and smiled.

'So this is a nice place,' she said, turning slightly to look around his apartment and deciding that actually nice was way too bland a word for the incredible vision that met her eyes.

It was open plan, the kitchen partly cut off by a wide breakfast bar giving way to a dining area, which then flowed into a vast and comfortable-looking sitting room containing a wide deep sofa, several well-worn armchairs and a coffee table piled high with magazines.

Bookshelves lined the far wall and sagged beneath the weight of the dozens of books that were stacked upon them. Light spilled in through the floor-to-ceiling windows filling the room with light and shadows. Plants sat on every horizontal surface and art hung on every vertical one.

It was the sort of flat a girl could get very cosy in, thought Nicky, if that was her intention, which in *her* case, of course, it wasn't.

'I like it,' he said abruptly.

'You like plants,' she observed.

'I do.'

'It's spacious,' she murmured and wondered where his bedroom was. 'Light. Airy.'

'And remarkably close to my office,' he said dryly.

'How handy.'

'Isn't it?'

And that seemed to be that for small talk, Nicky realised as she swung her gaze back to him and they lapsed into a tense little silence.

The seconds ticked by and Rafael just stood there looking at her with those penetrating green eyes and that unfathomable expression, barely moving a muscle, and she just stood there helplessly staring back, the tension inside her winding tighter and tighter as the heat flowing though her picked up speed and intensity.

As their gazes held the silence stretched, began to thicken and sizzle with electricity until it finally became unbearable and Nicky came to the conclusion that as he appeared to have no intention of doing anything to break it, she was going to have to.

'So,' she said, blinking to snap herself out of it and smiling brightly, 'I guess you must be wondering what I'm doing here.'

One dark eyebrow lifted. 'I can't imagine it was solely to discuss the weather, the architectural features of my flat and my interest in plants,' he said, sounding impressively bored.

'You'd be right,' Nicky answered, completely undeterred by his indifference because she was on a mission and nothing was going to sway her from it.

'So?'

'Well, firstly I just wanted to say that I thought you leaving without saying goodbye was rather on the rude side.'

He shrugged. 'Like I said in my note, I had work. But you're right. I apologise.'

'Accepted. Secondly, I wanted to see if you were all right.'

This time both eyebrows shot up. 'Why wouldn't I be?'

'When I last spoke to Gaby I rather got the feeling she'd like to do you some harm.'

Something flickered in the depths of his eyes but it was gone before she could identify it.

'As you can see I'm perfectly fine. And while I appreciate your concern,' he added, clearly not appreciating it at all, 'a phone call would have done.'

'True on both counts,' she agreed with a brief nod. 'But a phone call would certainly not have done for the main reason I'm here.'

'Which is?'

Deciding that neither a subtle approach nor skirting around the issue would break through such determined lack of emotion, but that getting straight to the point might at least provoke some sort of reaction, Nicky took a deep breath. 'Right,' she said, pulling her shoulders back, straightening her spine and looking him straight in the eye. 'Well. You see, the thing is, I'd like to give that kiss another try.'

When he'd looked through the spyhole and seen Nicky standing on his doorstep, smiling and waving, distorted but still lovely, Rafael had thought that someone somewhere really had it in for him. That he must have done something really terrible in a former life, because this was the second time she'd surprised him at a door and, while she might not have been armed with *Don Quijote* on this occasion, her impact had been no less devastating.

Which was why, feeling as if the whole sodding universe was conspiring against him, he'd been momentarily tempted to tiptoe back and hole up in his office in the hope that she'd give up and leave. However, given the not-particularly-subtle way he'd walked to the door, he'd realised that unfortunately that wasn't an option so he'd had to brace himself and let her in.

To a man whose defences weren't as indestructible as his now were, Nicky Sinclair, tanned, relaxed and smiling, wrapped in a dress that showed off her lovely curves and shod in high peep-toe wedges that added inches to her already willowy height, might have presented the ultimate temptation.

But not to him. Oh, no. Distance and time had given him ample opportunity to fortify his defences and they were now sky-high, unbreachable and as solid as rock, so he was immune.

If his detached approach felt like harder work than it should have done, it was merely that he'd been briefly thrown off balance by her unexpected appearance. And if he'd nearly dropped his glass when she'd mentioned trying the kiss again, well, that was simply surprise at her boldness, nothing more.

'What kiss?' he asked nonchalantly, aware she was waiting for some kind of response.

Nicky shot him a look that suggested she wasn't convinced by his nonchalance one little bit, and arched an eyebrow. 'The one you gave me that last Sunday. The one by the pool.'

'Oh, that kiss,' he said as if it hadn't been on his mind constantly over the last fortnight.

'That's the one. So what do you think?'

'About trying it again?'

She nodded.

'Well, it's an interesting proposal,' he said, and shot her the hint of a cool and with any luck condescending smile, 'and a very flattering one, of course, but I'm afraid it's out of the question.'

Nicky tilted her head and bit her lip as she stared at him. 'Out of the question?'

He nodded. 'Out of the question.'

'Why?'

Good point. Why was it out of the question? he wondered, his gaze dropping for a split second to that lip before he snapped back to his senses and dragged his eyes back up. 'I'm rather surprised you'd want to.'

'Are you?'

Now *she* was the one who sounded surprised, and frankly that was odd because surely she couldn't have forgotten her total lack of interest in that kiss. 'You didn't seem all that keen at the time,' Rafael said, and reminded himself that whatever it was that was stabbing at his chest it couldn't be hurt because he'd got over all that weeks ago.

'No, but things have changed.'

'How convenient.'

'Not entirely, but is my perceived lack of interest your only objection?'

'Not by a long shot.'

'Then what else is it?'

For a second he just stood there looking at her, his mind boggling. God, where to start? 'For one thing *I* don't particularly want to.' That was as good a place as any.

'Why not?'

'It wasn't exactly a success the last time we tried it,' he drawled, thinking that that was at least partly the truth. 'So why on earth would I want to go through it again?'

'It would be better this time. I guarantee it.'

'There isn't going to be a this time.' And he could guarantee *that*.

There was a brief pause while she glanced at his jaw,

his shoulders, and lifted her eyebrows. 'Are you absolutely certain about that?' she said eventually. 'Because you look remarkably tense for a man who isn't interested in experimenting with one harmless little kiss.'

Harmless? Kissing Nicky? Hah. Rafael forced his shoulders to loosen up and then shrugged. 'Well, I'm not,' he said as if he couldn't be more relaxed. 'I, for one, have moved on.'

She nodded and bit her lip. 'Ah.'

'As I told you at the time my attraction to you was mercifully short-lived, and I got over it days ago.'

'Oh, yes. I remember. It was an aberration. The sun or the wine or something.'

Now it was his turn to arch an eyebrow because she sounded so continually sceptical and somehow knowing that it was seriously beginning to wind him up. 'Is it really that hard for you to believe your charms aren't irresistible?'

'Of course it isn't.' She regarded him thoughtfully and as she did so an odd thread of trepidation began to wind through him. 'But if you're not interested, as you claim, if you're no longer attracted to me, and if that kiss was so unimportant, why for the last ten minutes have you been staring at my mouth as if desperate to feel it beneath yours again?'

The foundations of his defences wobbled, and Rafael set his jaw to hold back the sudden burst of desire that he'd managed to convince himself he'd obliterated but was now pounding away at them. 'I haven't.'

'You have.'

'Must be a trick of the light.'

'Right,' she said with a slow nod. 'And I suppose the way your eyes are darkening, the way you're clenching your fist and that muscle hammering in your jaw must be tricks of the light too?' Her gaze dropped to the zip of his shorts behind which he was helplessly swelling and hardening. 'Not to mention the way your—'

'OK, enough,' he said, and slammed his glass down on the counter, suddenly so sick of the way his body, his senses and everything about this conversation were so out of control that he couldn't hold back. 'Maybe I am attracted to you.'

'Aha, I knew it,' she said with a triumphant little smile.

'Maybe I would like to kiss you again,' he continued, now on an unstoppable roll. 'Maybe I would like to drag you to the floor, strip you naked and bury myself inside you, but it's not going to happen.' About that he was absolutely certain. 'Nor am I going to let you kiss me, however seductively you try and dress up your request.'

For a second Nicky just looked at him, that damnably distracting mouth dropping open in shock at his outburst. 'But why ever not?' she said, her breathing ragged and her cheeks pink.

'Because you're not well,' he said tightly.

Her eyebrows shot up. 'What?'

'You're not well.'

She frowned. 'Have you been speaking to Gaby?'

'Yes.'

'What did she say?'

'That you needed a rest.'

'Which I've now had,' she said, taking a step towards him. 'Yes, I'll admit that I haven't been all that great, and my lack of response to you initially was part of it, but I'm better now. Much better.'

As if that made any difference, he thought, wishing he could take a giant step back and get out of her mind-scrambling orbit. 'I'm delighted to hear it,' he muttered roughly.

'So much so that over the last couple of weeks I've found myself thinking about you. About that kiss.' She paused and tilted her head. 'And whenever I did there was this kind of spark. Right here.' She splayed her hand low on her abdomen.

Rafael focused on a huge arrangement of flowers sitting on the breakfast bar to her right. 'Good for you.'

'It was. It is. And it could be good for both of us because now there's more than just a spark.'

'You could spontaneously combust and it wouldn't bother me one little bit.' Were those dahlia pinnatas?

'I feel I'm about to.'

'That's your prerogative.' They were, and if he wasn't much mistaken there were some spathiphyllum wallisii in there too. He looked a little harder. Yep. Definitely spathiphyllum wallisii.

Nicky let out an exasperated sigh. 'Rafael, what *is* your problem?'

He reluctantly dragged his gaze back to her and pushed his hands through his hair. 'You're a friend of Gaby's,' he stated flatly.

A pause. 'And?'

'And I don't get involved with friends of any of my sisters.'

'Why on earth not?'

'I did it once and it didn't work out well.'

'What happened?'

God, what hadn't happened? 'I married her.'

'Oh.'

'Quite,' he bit out. 'It went wrong and in the ensuing mess I nearly lost my sister as well as my wife. Do you really think I'd want to risk that happening again?'

'Do you really think it would?'

'I've no idea, but it could and I have no intention of putting it to the test. So forget it. Just forget it.'

Nicky slowly tapped her mouth with her index finger as she presumably considered his position. 'Look, Rafael,' she said eventually, pulling her shoulders back and fixing him with a disconcertingly probing look. 'Aren't you rather over-

analysing this? I'm not suggesting we get married or anything. Or even really get involved in a relationship. Heaven
forbid, that's the last thing I want. All I'm suggesting is a
kiss.'

Just a kiss? Was she nuts? He let out a sharp laugh. 'Really? Do you honestly think it would stop there?'

'Well, OK,' she said with a grin, 'if we're being honest,
I'm hoping not. I'm hoping that if the kiss works out well
then maybe we can take things further.'

'Further's the problem,' he all but snapped.

'Why? When is an afternoon of hot sex ever a problem?'

'When it gets complicated.'

'It won't,' she said firmly. 'It never does with me. Look,
now I've got my health back I'm not interested in anything
permanent, truly. So neither you nor your relationship with
Gaby are under any threat whatsoever from me.'

She walked over to him, smiled up at him, desire blazing in the blue-grey depths of her eyes, and put her hand on
his chest. 'Come on, Rafael,' she said softly and his vision
blurred. 'Haven't you wondered what it would be like? A
proper kiss. With *both* of us involved…'

Rafael felt as if he'd been thumped in the gut. Her prox-
imity blew all rational thought from his head and left it
empty of everything except harsh clamouring need. His skin
beneath her hand burned and his head pounded. He *had*
wondered what it would be like. Endlessly. And that was
precisely the trouble.

'Honestly, it's just one little kiss,' she said, her hand sliding higher, curving round his neck and threading through
his hair. 'How can one little kiss hurt?'

Beneath the onslaught of her scent, her warmth and her
innate sensuality those cracked and weakened foundations
crumbled, and down crashed his defences.

As they lay in smithereens at his feet once more Rafael

knew he didn't stand a chance. That since the moment he'd seen her through the spyhole he'd *never* stood a chance. He'd tried, but Nicky had battered down every one of his objections with logic and one smouldering smile after another, and now the pressure of wanting her was just too much.

There'd be time for explanations and regret and the chance to figure out what the hell was happening later. But right now he was drowning in need and he couldn't resist any longer.

With a strange sense that somehow this had been inevitable from the moment they'd met, Rafael gave up and gave in. 'Come here,' he muttered, and yanked her into his arms.

CHAPTER TEN

Oh, THANK GOD for that, thought Nicky as Rafael crushed her against him and slammed his mouth down on hers.

She'd known it would be tough to convince him that kissing her again was a good idea, but she'd never imagined it was going to be *that* hard. Goodness, the man was stubborn.

For a moment back there she'd feared her seduction skills were so rusty he'd never crack because she'd hurled everything she had at him and he'd just stood there firing back all those reasons why he wasn't going to kiss her, tight-jawed and as implacable as rock.

Well, almost as implacable as rock, she amended, her head beginning to swim as desire swirled around inside her, because she'd finally broken through all that idiotic denial, the not particularly convincing aloofness and all those baffling objections and, boy, was she glad she had.

Gone was the rigidly stoical Rafael of seconds ago, all buttoned up and resistant, and here was the man by the pool. Six feet three inches of wild and uncontrollable passion.

Her lips parted and as he pushed his tongue between them she groaned and sank against him. One of his arms wrapped itself around her waist and he buried his other hand in her hair, in an exact imitation of how he'd kissed her before but with one crucial difference.

And that was her response. There was nothing cold and

numb about that this time. His tongue touched hers, and she jerked as if electrocuted. Sparks shot straight through her and her blood began to sizzle. Heat pooled in her pelvis and spread throughout her body like a fever.

As they kissed the heat intensified and her insides began to burn as if a thousand fires had sprung to flame in the pit of her stomach.

Unable to help herself, Nicky moaned. Oh, how she'd missed this. This heady feeling of wanting. Of being wanted. Of the delirious desperation that intense need caused. She'd missed the feeling of drowning in desire, the unstoppable thundering of her heart and the giddy aching of her body.

For the first time in weeks she felt truly alive. Vibrant and on fire, and she pressed herself closer, wrapped her arms tighter, and kissed him back even more fiercely.

After what felt like hours, they broke off and she stared up at Rafael and blinked, fairly reeling at the strength of her reaction to him. His eyes were glittering, dark with desire, his breathing was ragged and she could feel his heart thundering against her. As it seemed he couldn't move or speak either she thought that perhaps he was as stunned as she was, and the knowledge sent primitive satisfaction surging through her.

'Well?' she murmured huskily.

He blinked, frowned, and then gave his head a quick shake. 'Well, what?'

'Didn't I guarantee it would be better this time?'

He blew out a soft shaky breath. 'You did.'

'And?'

'It was better.'

There was nothing wrong with better, thought Nicky, but the imp inside her, the one who'd been slumbering away for weeks now, was waking up. It yawned and rubbed its eyes and made her say with a coquettishness that she didn't usually go in for, 'Just better?'

'Much better.' His mouth curved into a faint smile and he raised his eyebrows. 'Why? Think you can improve?'

'Oh, there's always room for improvement,' she murmured and lifted her head for another divine kiss.

And this time when their mouths met Nicky's brain well and truly went AWOL, because within seconds Rafael had taken control and was angling her head and deepening the kiss and sliding his hand up her side as he kissed her.

His hand curved round her breast and settled, and at the feel of it caressing her achingly sensitive flesh she sighed into his mouth. He brushed his thumb over her nipple, sending more of those tiny electric shocks skidding through her, and she melted against him.

Oh, this was heavenly, she thought dazedly. Absolutely heavenly. Instinctively she tightened her arms around his neck and tilted her pelvis against his erection and rubbed. He groaned and pulled her even closer, kissed her even harder and blew her mind.

By the time they broke for breath this time her bones had dissolved and she was glad he had some kind of hold on her because otherwise she'd have collapsed into a puddle of lust on the floor.

'God, I'd love to see how we can improve on that,' she said shakily, and thought that she doubted it was possible because how could you perfect perfection?

He brushed a lock of her hair back and tucked it behind her ear. 'Would you?'

The oddly tender gesture coupled with the hint of promise in his voice and the suddenly wicked glint that appeared in his eye shot her pulse so far through the roof and stole her voice so totally that all she could do was nod.

He let her go and nudged her gently back. 'Then take off your dress.'

A great boulder of desire rolled the length of her body, nearly wiping out her knees, and she swallowed hard. 'Now?' she breathed, and inwardly winced at the way he'd evidently turned her brain to mush because was he really talking about next week?

He gave her a slow smouldering smile that had her stomach flipping like a pancake. 'Now.'

How could she do anything but comply when she was so completely spellbound by him and the dizzying effect he had on her?

Everything but him and the way he was looking at her faded into a blur. As she slipped out of her shoes, her hands went to her side of their own accord and she slid the zip of her dress down and with Rafael watching her every move so closely Nicky was aware of her body in a way she never had been before.

The whisper of her zip sounded abrasively loud in the eerie silence of the afternoon. The soft cotton of her dress brushing against her skin sent tiny shivers scuttling down her spine, and her fingers trembled a little as she slipped the straps off her shoulders and let the dress fall to the floor in a pool of pale yellow. Her heart reverberated like a kettle drum and her blood roared in her ears as she watched Rafael swallow once, then slowly run his gaze over her nearly naked body.

Beneath his scrutiny, a shudder rippled through her and then she went so hot she wouldn't have been surprised to look down and find that the lace of her strapless bra and knickers had gone up in flames.

'What now?' she asked, perfectly happy to have him take charge when it made her feel like this.

'Sit down.' His voice was satisfyingly hoarse and she

smiled at the thought that despite his attempt to resist her, he was as much at the mercy of this as she was.

'Where?' she asked, because the only chairs she could make out in her very fuzzy peripheral vision were the kitchen bar stools and they didn't look nearly sturdy enough for what she hoped was about to happen.

He scanned the living space. 'The sofa, I think.'

With her pulse kicking with anticipation, she smiled, then turned and made her way over to the wide, deep chocolate-brown sofa, feeling her body moving languidly and her hips sashaying in a way that had nothing to do with any conscious thought on her part and everything to do with a primitively innate desire to attract.

She sat down before her knees could give way and looked up at him. 'How do you want me?'

'Sit back.'

With desire and heat making the blood racing through her veins sluggish and her limbs heavy, Nicky languorously sank back against the soft velvet and inched her knees open a fraction.

'Is that better?' she said huskily.

'Much.'

'So what are you doing still over there?'

'Contemplating exactly where to start.'

As her mouth went dry and heat pooled between her legs Nicky thought that he'd started already. 'Will you be long?'

'I might be.'

'Why?'

'I've just discovered a hitherto latent fascination with revenge.'

She shivered deliciously. 'Revenge?'

He nodded. 'And I think I could be getting a taste for it.'

'Are you planning to make me pay for that disaster of a first kiss?' she said a little raggedly.

'I might be,' he said and the look in his eye told her that there was no 'might' about it.

Wicked excitement spun through her. 'How?'

'By making you beg.'

Oh, heavens. 'I've never begged for anything in my life.'

'You will.'

Her heart thumped so hard her ribs ached. And then, just when she didn't think she could stand the tension much longer, he pushed himself off the counter and began to prowl towards her, not taking his eyes off her as he approached.

He came to a stop in front of her, loomed over her for a moment and then dropped to his knees. He pushed her legs apart and inched forwards and her excitement ratcheted up so dizzyingly it was all she could do not to grab him and pull him first up and then down on top of her. Achingly slowly he leaned into her and the spicy scent of him wound up her nose into her head and made a mess of her brain.

When his mouth finally brushed over hers, Nicky moaned and nearly passed out with relief because for a moment she'd thought she was going to have to start begging right there and then.

But he didn't linger. Instead he moved his mouth down over her chin, her neck and the skin of her upper chest, leaving tiny trails of fire wherever it touched, and at the same time he slid his hands up her thighs. The muscles beneath his fingers quivered and the skin beneath his mouth burned and then his teeth grazed her nipple beneath the lace of her bra and she gasped.

As he tugged her hips forwards and carried on kissing his way down her body Nicky closed her eyes and let her head drop back because it was all getting too much for her poor battered senses and, unlike some of her previous lovers, Rafael didn't seem to need instruction.

Quite the contrary, she thought briefly as he dotted a

trail of kisses over her stomach and then lower, and ran his tongue along the edge of her knickers. He knew exactly what he was doing.

And then she gave up thinking altogether in favour of biting her lip and arching her back and clenching her fists against the cushions to stop herself grabbing his head and pushing it where she so desperately wanted his mouth.

She whimpered and felt him smile against her skin and then he was lifting her hips, hooking his thumbs over the sides of her knickers and drawing back to slide them down her legs. He pulled them off and began stroking and kissing his way up over the inside of one of her knees, up along her inner thigh and then he was there. Right at the heart of her where she was burning and aching and so, so hot. He spread her legs even further apart, exposing her completely, and she let out an involuntary little moan. And then just when she thought she might be ready to beg after all, he licked along the length of her and a burst of pleasure exploded inside her.

Holding her in place, he licked and sucked and nibbled and stroked and within seconds Nicky's head was swimming and her body was on fire and all her senses zoomed in on his tongue and the chaos it was creating.

After such a long time of nothing she was a writhing mass of sensation. As he continued to lay siege to her body shudders racked her. Need clawed at her insides. Her muscles filled with tension.

He slipped a finger, then two, into her wet heat, found her g-spot with deadly accuracy, and what with the relentless onslaught of his tongue, the feel of his fingers inside her and the ecstasy spinning out of control deep within her, it was all just too much.

Far too soon everything tangled into one great jumble of feeling, soaring and swelling until it hit a peak and, with his name on her lips, she shattered, breaking wide apart and spinning off into delirious oblivion.

When the stars eventually stopped exploding behind her eyelids, when her heart finally slowed and when the strength eventually returned to her limbs, Nicky let out a long shuddery breath and opened her eyes.

'Been a while?'

She lifted her head and glanced down to find Rafael staring up at her, his eyes glittering with desire, satisfaction and a hint of surprise.

'You could say that,' she said huskily, then added because it seemed appropriate, 'Thanks.'

'It was my pleasure.'

'No, no, the pleasure was all mine. Literally.' And embarrassingly, she thought, feeling a blush steal into her cheeks at the memory of how abandoned, how vocal she'd been.

Rafael grinned. 'Yes, well, don't worry. There'll be plenty of time to even up the score.'

'You mean there's more?' she asked, widening her eyes with disingenuous innocence as a ribbon of fresh desire wound through her.

'Much more.'

Nicky smiled and stretched. 'I'm glad to hear it because you haven't even got naked yet.'

He looked down over her once again with that heated gaze and her stomach melted. 'Technically neither have you,' he said.

Arching an eyebrow and giving him a saucy little smile, Nicky reached behind her back, unclipped her bra and tossed it over the back of her sofa. 'Situation remedied,' she declared. 'And now, in the interest of fairness, it's your turn.'

Rafael's gaze dropped to her breasts and a muscle began to hammer in his jaw. 'Since you're so good at it,' he murmured, 'why don't you do it?'

'Bedroom?'

'Conventional. Who'd have thought?'

She shrugged. 'What can I say? I'm a fan of horizontal surfaces and space.' Although upright on the sofa wasn't such a bad alternative.

'In that case,' he said, holding out his hands, taking hers and pulling them both to their feet, 'the bedroom's this way.'

CHAPTER ELEVEN

OH, YES, THOUGHT Nicky, standing beside the bed, letting her gaze drift over Rafael and wondering where she was going to start. Coming to Madrid had been *such* a good idea and she was going to have so much fun with him because for this afternoon at least he was all hers, and she felt like a kid in a sweet shop, her fingers itching to delve and her mouth watering with the need to sample the wares.

'Are you just going to stand there and look?' said Rafael, and she looked up to see his face was dark and tight. 'Because I am this close—' he held up his thumb and forefinger a millimetre apart '—to tossing you onto the bed and ravishing you, and, believe me, finesse will not feature heavily.'

And there'd be nothing wrong with that, she thought, her heart jumping as desire shot through her all over again. But now that she'd got her mojo back—and how—she wanted to indulge every newly awakened sense.

So with her breath catching in her throat she put her hands on his stomach and slid them up, lifting his T-shirt as she did so and feeling his muscles twitch beneath her palms. He raised his arms to help her and she stood on tiptoe to pull the T-shirt over his head and up over his arms. She let it drop to the floor and then ran her hands back down his lowering arms and across his shoulders and then down over the broad tanned expanse of his chest.

Unable to resist, she leaned forwards and flicked her tongue over his nipple. Rafael inhaled sharply and she could feel his body tighten. With restraint. With desire.

'God, I'd forgotten how tantalising undressing a man could be,' she murmured.

'Done it often?'

'Once or twice.' Although never with someone quite like him. Relieving him of his clothes had to be one of life's greatest secret pleasures because he was physically quite magnificent.

Swallowing hard, she moved her hands down, undid his belt, the button of his shorts and then slid down the zip, relishing every glorious second.

And to think that that day he'd kissed her by the pool she'd had ample opportunity to admire the body on display. To ogle and want and touch. And she'd ignored it. What a waste.

Well, she wasn't ignoring it now. And she wasn't going to waste a second.

She slid her hands beneath the waistband of his boxers and moaned in anticipation as she eased them and his shorts over the thick, hard erection that she could feel beneath. He stepped out of them and she took a step back to simply admire. God, his body was incredible. It was all lean, hard muscle and taut restrained power and she couldn't wait to have the full force of it unleashed on her.

'Lie down,' he said in a voice that wasn't altogether steady.

Nicky's heart thumped madly as she did as he said and lay back on the bed, because, oh, there was definitely something to be said for a gorgeous man who knew how and when to use his power and liked to be in control.

And right now, with the way his eyes were burning over her, she was quite willing to submit herself to whatever delicious torment he had planned. There'd be plenty of time for payback later, she decided, and felt a wide wanton smile steal across her face.

'That smile looks dangerous,' he said, his eyes blazing down at her.

'Could be.'

'Sirens,' he muttered. 'I'm doomed.'

'What?'

'Sirens.'

'What about them?' she said, and stretched in what she hoped was an enticing manner because there was drawing things out and indulging her senses and then there was just plain being sadistic, and the way she was lying spreadeagled on the bed while he still remained upright and beside it definitely fell into the latter category.

'They had a tendency to lure sailors to their deaths with their song,' he said.

'Lucky you're not a sailor and I can't sing, then, isn't it?'

'You have plenty of other attractions.'

'So are you just going to stand there and look at them?' she asked, recalling his earlier words to her and deciding to hurry things up a bit. 'Or are you planning to do the decent thing and join me, because I am this close—' she held up her thumb and forefinger a millimetre apart '—to pulling you onto this bed and ravishing you.' She paused and smiled and batted her eyelashes up at him. 'And, believe me, finesse will not feature heavily.'

That seemed to do the trick. Rafael let out a strangled groan, jerked forwards and, planting his hands either side of her head, came down heavily on top of her. At the sudden urgency of his actions Nicky's breath shot from her lungs and lust spun through her.

'You know, I'm coming to the conclusion that finesse is vastly overrated,' he said roughly.

'You have no idea how glad I am to hear you think so,'

she said softly, loving the feel of his weight on top of her and wrapping a leg around his waist.

And then his mouth was on hers and she couldn't remember what she'd been glad about because his hands were in her hair, his tongue was in her mouth and both were rendering her to a mindless tangle of electricity, desire and delicious, delicious tension.

She ran her hands over the tight muscles of his shoulders and his back and dug her nails in, which took the kiss to another, more frenzied, more desperate dimension in which clashing teeth, melding moans and writhing limbs dominated.

Her head was so foggy, her brain so utterly destroyed, she was only dimly aware of Rafael pulling one hand from her hair and sliding it down her neck and then over the agonisingly sensitive skin of her upper chest.

But when it came to a rest on her breast all that electricity, desire and tension shot through the roof. Nicky groaned into his mouth and arched her back as his hand cupped her and he rubbed his thumb back and forth over her nipple and a burst of white-hot pleasure exploded deep inside her.

He dragged his mouth away and shifted a little, and she gulped in a shaky breath as it closed over her other nipple.

Biting her lip to stop herself from crying out at the stabs of ecstasy that were jabbing at her, she pressed her fingers into his head and tilted her hips to grind into his erection. She writhed. She whimpered. She simply couldn't help it.

'Ready to beg yet?' he said hoarsely against her breast.

God, probably, she thought dazedly, but in a bit because she wanted more and could take more. 'Not nearly,' she said, and then added in the hope it would make him double his already sensational efforts, 'You'll have to try far harder than that.'

So he did.

His mouth resumed its devastating assault on her breast and his hand slid lower and lower until it reached the juncture of her thighs and then his fingers were parting her and sliding into her and the feeling was so electrifying she would have jackknifed upright had he not been pressing her down.

He stroked her, relentlessly, expertly and her insides wound so tightly she felt they might snap at any moment. Heat coiled in the pit of her stomach. Tremors began to rack her body and shivers raced through her veins as the excitement swelled and spread into every cell of her body. She was hovering on the brink, a nanosecond away from splintering, clenching around his fingers and hurtling off into oblivion when suddenly he stilled and his head lifted.

Nicky groaned in protest as her orgasm instantly ebbed. 'Why are you stopping?' she said, her voice rough and raspy.

His green eyes gleamed down at her. 'Beg me,' he muttered.

What? Oh, his timing was good, she thought as a stab of such intense longing shot through her that she nearly did as he asked. Or very very bad, depending on your point of view. She didn't know which hers was.

'Sadist,' she murmured.

'Beg me,' he said again.

'No.'

'Masochist.'

'You'll pay for this,' she said, reaching down, taking him in her hand and stroking. She felt him tense and shudder so she rubbed her thumb across the tip and gently squeezed.

'I have a feeling we both will,' he said raggedly, stopping her hand, then abruptly rolling slightly and twisting away.

Nicky watched as he rummaged around in the drawer of the bedside table and pulled out a condom. He ripped open the packet, slipped it on and then he was back on top of her, his eyes blazing down at her and his erection nudging at her entrance. Hovering. Waiting. Wanting her completely and utterly at his mercy, which she was.

She opened her legs wider. Tilted her hips higher. And then he was driving into her with a rough groan and she thought that she was about to die and go to heaven.

'Oh…' she said, letting out a long shuddery breath as she felt him fill her.

'Incredible,' he muttered, going utterly still for a second before beginning to move. Deliberately slowly, ruthlessly measuredly and maddeningly in control.

And while there was certainly a time for languid and leisurely, right now she was in the mood for fast and frantic because the friction was becoming unbearable, the tension excruciating, and the pleasure relentless, and it wasn't enough. The climax that had remained so tantalisingly out of reach when he'd stopped and asked her to beg still hovered at the edges of her consciousness.

He was holding it off, holding them both back, and no matter how much she writhed and rubbed against him he didn't relent. She pulled his head down for a searing kiss and felt sparks shoot through her at the touch of his lips, his tongue, but none of it made the slightest difference. The only thing that all her efforts achieved was her own torment because with each tilt of her hips, with each twist and turn of her body and with each kiss she simply grew more and more frenzied until she was way beyond the point of any kind of control.

'Oh, God,' she mumbled, hearing the desperation in her voice and not caring one little bit. 'Please…'

And then a second later his control seemed to dissolve and a wildness took over his movements and Nicky found she cared even less, because gone was maddeningly slow and ruthlessly measured, and he was now thrusting into her over and over again, going deeper, harder, faster until she didn't think she could bear it any longer.

The delirium inside her escalated with each thrust, sweeping her up in it, higher and higher until the great ball of pressure inside her erupted and she hurtled over the edge, her body exploding into a thousand tiny fireworks of ecstasy.

She shook, convulsed and trembled in his arms, the tremors shuddering through her nearly breaking her apart and then she felt him bury himself deep inside her one last time, groan and pulsate into her, and unbelievably she came all over again.

For several long, long minutes neither of them moved. Nicky wouldn't have been able to even if Rafael hadn't collapsed on top of her because she felt utterly sated and utterly drained. As weak as a kitten, and quite extraordinarily good.

'Wow,' she managed once her breathing had eased, her heart rate had slowed and her surroundings had swum back into focus.

'Quite.' Even with his mouth muffled by her shoulder, Rafael sounded as stunned as she was.

'What was that?'

Gently easing out of her, he rolled to one side and propped himself up on an elbow. 'One harmless little kiss apparently.'

She looked up at him and slowly smiled. 'Ah, but it didn't hurt, did it?'

'The kisses didn't,' he said raggedly. 'However the damage to my back might be irreparable.'

'Sorry,' she said, too happy revelling in the aftermath of what had been the most glorious sex of her life to feel in the slightest bit apologetic. 'Is it that bad?'

'Not that bad. And I think I can live with it. Especially since you begged so nicely.'

She jerked her gaze to his and arched an eyebrow at the teasing glint in his eyes. 'I did not beg.'

'Yes, you did. I remember it clearly.'

'I pleaded. There's a difference.'

'You think?'

His grin was too smug to ignore. 'I'll show you.'

'How?'

Giving him a deliberately smouldering smile, Nicky pushed him onto his back, climbed on top of him and watched with satisfaction as a flicker of wariness leapt in his eyes.

'You'll see,' she said, and began to slide down his body.

'You know, you're absolutely right,' said Rafael quite a while later when he was able to think again. 'There is a difference.'

Nicky glanced up and grinned. 'Told you.'

'Feeling smug?'

'A little.'

And actually she had every right to, he thought, because frankly the afternoon had been astounding. When he'd initially pulled her into his arms he'd had the feeling that they'd be good together, but nothing could have prepared him for the explosive way they'd responded to each other. Over and over again she'd come apart in his arms and beneath his mouth, and he'd shattered in and beneath hers more times than he could count. It was truly staggering.

Now it was dusk and she was sitting cross-legged in his bed wearing one of his T-shirts and eating a tortilla he'd whipped up, tousled haired, sleepy-eyed and looking thoroughly ravished, and with any luck the night would be equally astonishing because unbelievably he wanted her again.

As the desire that had never really gone away surged through him for the dozenth time this afternoon Rafael felt himself harden and stabbed his fork into a piece of tortilla.

What was it about Nicky that made him lose such control and forget about everything but her? Where had all those thoughts of revenge come from? And as for wanting to make her beg, what the hell had that been all about?

The need to possess her, to make her succumb, had been all-consuming, and, for someone who'd always been so focused and in control when it came to sex, the realisation that all it took was a gorgeous woman, weeks of frustration and scorching chemistry to derail him so spectacularly like that was kind of harrowing.

'And tired,' said Nicky, yanking Rafael out of his thoughts in time for him to see her smothering a yawn and stretching languidly. 'You've worn me out. It's a good thing I stocked up on rest at the *cortijo.*'

And that was another thing, he thought as the comment she'd made earlier about not being well flashed into his head and a wave of guilt washed over him. Forget the mental gymnastics *he* was going through. What about the extremely physical ones he'd spent the afternoon subjecting her to?

He swore softly beneath his breath. Nicky had been ill and never mind that everything they'd done had been entirely mutual, he should have taken more care. Better still, he should have held his ground and resisted her in the first place, but there was little use in beating himself up about that again.

'Rafael?' she asked, the tinge of concern in her voice making him feel even worse. 'Are you all right?'

'Are you?'

She blinked and shot him a dazzling smile that slowly flipped his stomach. 'Of course I am. I feel fabulous. Why do you ask?'

'You said you hadn't been very well.'

She raised her eyebrows. 'True, but I also said I'd recovered. As I think we've just admirably demonstrated.' She frowned. 'I hope you don't think you hurt me or anything.'

Rafael stiffened with resolve because he'd let too much

slide and he wasn't about to let this go. 'If you've been ill, can you blame me?'

There was a pause, then she set her fork down and looked at him, pinning him to the mattress with those stormy grey-blue eyes of hers. 'OK,' she said, linking her fingers in her lap and leaning forwards earnestly. 'Here's the thing. Yes, I haven't been particularly well, but neither have I been exactly ill.'

As his once sharp but now apparently addled brain tried to work out what she meant and failed, Rafael frowned. He'd had a first class education initially at public school in England, then at Cambridge and finally at Harvard, and he'd always assumed he was pretty much bilingual, but perhaps he'd been deluding himself all these years. Perhaps somewhere along the way he'd missed the lesson on nuance, because right now he couldn't work out what she was saying. 'I'm afraid you've lost me.'

'I nearly lost myself.'

'How?' he asked, now even more perplexed.

'Burnout.'

'Burnout?'

'That's right. Gaby diagnosed it a few weeks ago and I think she was right.'

The image of the Nicky he'd first met flashed though Rafael's head. She'd been pale and gaunt. Exhausted and troubled. Tense, prickly and on edge. And enveloped by that disturbing air of desolate defeat.

All classic signs of burnout, he realised, and all of which he'd seen before. Hell, he'd even got work because of it but it had never occurred to him that that was what Nicky had been suffering from. But then he'd been so caught up in wanting her and wondering why she didn't want him that little else *had* occurred to him.

'What caused it?' he said, and forced himself to focus on

her instead of barrelling off down the road of self-recrimination yet again.

She tilted her head and regarded him for a moment, as
if internally debating whether or not to tell him. Then she
straightened as if bracing herself, and for some reason his
chest tightened. 'Remember how I told you I was a photojournalist?'

He nodded and took a deep breath to ease the pressure.
'I looked you up on the Internet. Your work is incredible.'
Although actually incredible didn't begin to describe it. The
pictures she took were powerful, provocative, beautiful and
thought-provoking. He'd read that she'd won awards and as
he'd scrolled through the gallery on her website he'd been
able to see why.

She beamed. 'Thank you.' Then she sobered. 'Well, anyway, a year or so ago I was on assignment in the Middle
East, covering a demonstration about rights for women. It
was all going fine. Very peaceful and I got some excellent
shots. But then some men turned up—family members of
a few of the women, I found out later—and took exception.
Especially to me and my camera.'

He thought he heard her voice shake a little and the pressure in his chest returned. 'What happened then?'

Nicky sighed. 'To be honest I don't remember all that
much about it. One minute I was taking pictures, the next I
was surrounded and being jostled and pushed to the ground.
But I guess eventually my instinct for survival kicked in
because somehow I managed to escape and make my way
back to my hotel.'

Rafael felt his jaw clench. Why on earth had she put herself in such danger? Surely no photograph was worth risk-
ing one's life for?

'Of course I'd had training in how to deal with things
like that,' she continued, 'but it was the first time it had hap-

pened to me and, in all the panic, I kind of forgot everything I'd been taught.'

'Were you badly hurt?'

'Depends what you mean by badly. I only had a couple of broken ribs so I guess I got off pretty lightly really. My camera, however, suffered infinitely more. It was smashed to bits. Luckily, though, I'd managed to take out the memory card before they got hold of it.'

'It must have been terrifying.'

Nicky shrugged. 'It's not an experience I'm particularly keen to repeat, I admit. And I'm not a huge fan of crowds.'

'I'm not surprised. So is that what your nightmares are about?'

This time she didn't bother pretending she didn't know what he was talking about. 'Pretty much.' She added, 'Sometimes the details vary but only slightly. Lately though they've been getting fuzzier and I have them far less often than I used to so that's good. Anyway it all happened ages ago, and I'm fine about it. Really.'

Hmm. Was she? 'So where does the burnout come in?'

Nicky blinked and gave him a rueful smile. 'Oh, well, I was so determined to prove that what had happened hadn't affected me that I went a bit overboard on the work front.'

'Overboard?'

'Put it this way. I didn't so much get back on the horse as saddle it up and take it round the Grand National a couple of times. I started working every waking hour I had and barely stopped for breath.'

Rafael frowned. 'Was that sustainable?'

'No. I was hurtling from time zone to time zone so much that I had no idea whether it was morning or night. It played havoc on my sleep and eventually I just wore out. Even taking my camera out of its case ended up becoming a major task and that scared me witless because if I can't take photos

I don't know what else there is.' She ran a hand through her hair. 'I think I just kind of gave up. It was so tiring treading water, I simply stopped. And once I'd done that then I really began to sink.'

'That doesn't sound good,' he muttered, knowing it was an understatement but too mystified by all the stuff beginning to churn around inside him to respond with anything more sensible.

'No, well, it wasn't,' she said dryly, 'but it's why I ended up at your house. It's why when we met I was in a bit of a state. And it's why when you kissed me I couldn't respond, even though I desperately wanted to. When I told you that my lack of response to you wasn't you but me, I meant it. Along with everything else I'd lost all interest in sex. It was like I was dead inside.'

'But not any more.'

She grinned. 'Not any more. And I've been taking pictures again. Of your vineyard. Do you mind?'

Did he mind? God, it was the least he could offer after all she'd been through. After all he'd put her through, and not just this afternoon. 'Of course not.'

Her smile deepened and his stomach twisted. 'Great. Well, anyway, it turns out your sister is quite the psychiatrist because she was the one who decided a rest and a time-out to regroup was the answer and she was right. That *cortijo* of yours was exactly what I needed.'

No, what Nicky needed was looking after, Rafael decided darkly, because God, he'd thought he'd had a tough time of it lately, but, compared with what she'd been through, a merger, a handful of demanding relatives and a persistent ex were nothing. And she might act as if she was over what had happened but was she? Really?

'So what plans do you have next?' he asked, ignoring the little voice inside his head demanding to know where he thought he was going with this, because she might not really be over it and she might need looking after but he definitely wasn't the sort of person who should be getting involved.

She lifted her eyebrows. 'You mean beyond some more of that lovely restorative sex?'

'Beyond that.'

She blinked and shrugged. 'I don't know. I'm not very good at living beyond the present.'

'Well, I'm at a loose end… You're at a loose end… What would you say to tying our loose ends together for a while?'

She grinned. 'I'd say does that line really work?'

Rafael frowned because oddly enough it hadn't been a line. 'I have no idea. You tell me.'

CHAPTER TWELVE

APPARENTLY IT DID because a week later Nicky was back at the *cortijo* with Rafael, and she was loving every minute of it.

And why wouldn't she be when she was being so well attended to? she thought, feeling a sleepy satisfied smile spread across her face as she yawned and stretched gingerly so as not to wake Rafael, who was still asleep beside her.

Since they'd been back he'd been pretty much the perfect host. Not only had he made sure she was well fed and well rested, but he'd kept her entertained too. He'd taken her to the beach and taught her the basics of kite surfing. He'd driven her up into the coolness of the hills to a fabulous little restaurant overlooking a sparkling lake and fed her lobster. He'd spent an afternoon showing her round the vineyards and explaining how the *fino* she'd acquired quite a taste for was made. And then yesterday he'd asked her if she'd like to help with the harvest and they'd spent the day cutting away fat heavy bunches of grapes, until she couldn't bear her aching back any longer and had begged him for a massage.

As for the nights—and the siestas—well, those were something else. Nicky had always thought she'd had an active and relatively adventurous sex life but sleeping with Rafael took it to a whole new level. Over and over again she hit heights she'd never reached before, experiencing pleasure she hadn't known existed. The lavish attention he paid her body and the wild intensity with which he devoured her blew her mind every time.

She didn't regret telling him all about her recent history one little bit. Back then, sitting on his bed in Madrid in the wake of that extraordinary afternoon, it had felt like the ideal opportunity to test her emotional strength, and it had been everything she'd hoped for.

Opening up to him had been wonderfully liberating and that feeling of relief and freedom still lingered so she'd had no problem with answering the dozens of other questions he had about what had happened. She'd happily spilled out the details he'd asked for and at some point during the last week she'd felt something shift inside her. Something heavy dissipate. And she rather thought that at last—*finally*—she seemed to be getting over what had happened to her.

How she'd ever imagined that she and Rafael had nothing in common other than Gaby and a dislike of complicated relationships Nicky would never know. Apart from being astonishingly compatible in bed, they shared a love of the outdoors and travel. Of good food and hard work. Of books and art. Intrigued, she'd interrogated him about his fascination with plants and he'd been equally curious about her unconventional upbringing.

They seemed to be able to talk, laugh and argue about virtually everything under the sun. In fact pretty much the only thing that they *hadn't* talked about was his marriage, and it sat between them like the proverbial elephant in the room. Or at least *her* corner of the room because, while Rafael was no doubt perfectly happy to leave it alone, she was becoming quite obsessed with wanting to know all about it.

As she'd got to know him better, she'd found herself wondering what kind of husband he'd been, what his wife had been like, what kind of marriage they'd had and why it had failed. None of which she needed to know, of course, because she certainly wasn't interested in him—or anyone else for that matter—in a matrimonial kind of way, but that didn't stop her whiling away endless hours wondering.

And because she could never ask such intrusive questions her imagination had been working overtime. He'd be protective, she'd decided. Passionate. Loyal. And caring. Oh, he might like to make out that he was only interested in himself but that wasn't true at all, was it? Over the last few days she'd gathered plenty of evidence that contradicted *that* claim. She'd seen it in the way he'd provided food and water and shade for the temporary workers who'd been brought in to help with the harvest. In the way he'd frogmarched the housekeeper, Ana, to her room when she'd been stoically trying to carry on her duties through a streaming summer cold.

And in the way he'd kept a distant yet watchful eye on *her*.

Not that he'd needed to keep an eye on her because she was doing fine on her own, but that didn't stop warmth stealing through her whenever she glanced at him and caught him looking at her with what she thought might be concern and heat and something else that she was struggling to identify.

The warmth would have been worrying if she hadn't known perfectly well that she and Rafael wouldn't—couldn't—last. She hadn't been lying when she'd told him she wasn't interested in anything long-term; now she was back to her usual self, she fully intended to resume her old life and globetrot her way across the planet in the way she knew and loved.

Besides, they'd soon be going their separate ways. Once the summer was over Rafael would head back to Madrid and work, and she'd be back in Paris and lining up work of her own. And if that didn't sound quite as appealing as it should, well, that was just nervousness about having been out of the game for a while, nothing more.

Rafael stirred and Nicky frowned. Hmm. Maybe the fact

that this thing between them would inevitably come to an end—and sooner rather than later—was something she ought to keep in the forefront of her mind. She couldn't stay here for ever, and right now she might be having a great time but it wouldn't do to get lulled into a false sense of security, which would be all too easy to do seeing as this last week had been so idyllic.

She should probably stop spending quite so much time in his bed, she thought, carefully disentangling herself from the sheet and shifting away from him. In it she tended to lose all sense of perspective and reality and, while it was utterly lovely, getting used to it wouldn't do her any favours at all. Even if she wanted to, with the way she scooted around the world, living in hotel rooms and out of a suitcase, she simply couldn't afford to get used to anything.

Barely managing to resist the temptation to flop back and wake Rafael up in the most delicious way she could think of, Nicky was in the process of swinging her legs round when a hand snapped round her wrist and stopped her in her tracks.

'Where are you off to?' he said sleepily.

She twisted round and glanced down at him, drinking in the rumpled hair and sexy smile, and for a moment couldn't remember. 'I thought I might get up.'

He rubbed his eyes, gave his head a quick shake and shifted up onto his elbow. 'Why?'

'Because it's five in the afternoon.'

'So?' He stroked her wrist and her stomach all but disappeared.

Nicky swallowed and racked her brains for a reason to get up when there wasn't one. 'My feet are getting itchy,' she said even though they'd never felt less itchy.

'OK,' he said, sliding his hand up her arm and making goosebumps pop up all over her skin, 'so how about a trip into town?'

'That sounds great.'

'Then into town we'll go,' he murmured, and then pulled her down and back into his arms and gave her a kiss that frazzled her brain and made a mockery of her pathetic effort to resist him. 'Later.'

Quite a long time later, Rafael was sitting with Nicky at a table in a square in the centre of town, toying with the stem of his wine glass and wondering if he ought to be worried about what was going on here.

There were certainly things he *should* be worried about. Work or, rather, his lack of interest in it was one, for example. Nicky's friendship with his sister and its odd insignificance was another. Above all, he really ought to be concerned about the way that virtually anything that related to life beyond the physical and metaphorical boundaries of the vineyard simply didn't seem to matter.

Anything related to *real* life, in fact.

What was going on with Nicky wasn't real, he reminded himself, glancing over at her from behind his sunglasses and seeing a dreamy, wistful kind of smile curve her mouth. It couldn't last for ever, and nor did he want it to. Never mind that she was remarkably easy to be with. Never mind that she was fascinating. And never mind that night after night she blew his mind. She'd soon be going home, as would he, and he was absolutely fine with that.

So why did the thought of this being over and of her disappearing from his life for good leave such a bitter taste in his mouth? Why did it make his stomach twist and his chest squeeze? And when had the idea of going home started to sound quite so unappealing?

Rafael's fingers tightened around his glass and he shifted in his chair as it struck him that perhaps he wasn't quite as happy about the temporary nature of this thing with Nicky as he'd tried to convince himself.

Come to think of it, why did it have to be temporary anyway? Why couldn't they continue seeing each other even after they'd returned to their respective homes?

Nicky might have said she wasn't looking for a relationship but presumably she'd meant one that tied her to one place, that compromised her freedom. But over the last week he'd come to understand and respect her sense of wanderlust and he'd never ask that of her. Besides, why would he even want to when her independence, her self-sufficiency and her commitment to her work were among the things he most liked about her?

In that respect they were perfect for each other, so what would be wrong with a hot, steamy, long-distance affair? Nothing, as far as he could work out, so perhaps he ought to suggest it and see what she had to say...

'So what did your wife think of all this?'

Nicky's question yanked him out of his thoughts and he froze with shock at the unexpectedness of it. His wife? She wanted to talk about his *wife*? Now?

Forcing himself not to tense up, Rafael swivelled round to look at her. She was frowning and she'd gone a little pink and he got the impression that it was a question she hadn't intended to ask.

He wished she hadn't because the subject of his marriage wasn't one he cared to dwell on, but now she'd brought it up he could hardly pretend she hadn't, however much he might want to. He supposed he was lucky to have got away without having to discuss it for this long.

But never mind. It was fine. Just because she'd asked didn't mean he had to tell her anything other than the basic facts, did it?

'My wife?' he echoed.

'Well, your ex-wife,' she amended with a slight smile.

'She didn't think anything about this.'

Nicky frowned. 'What do you mean?'

'She never came down here.'

Her eyebrows shot up. 'What, never?'

'No,' he said coolly. 'I've only had the vineyard for five years and she was always more interested in city life anyway.'

'What was her name?'

'Marina.'

'And what was she like?'

'Blonde. Beautiful.'

'Naturally,' she said dryly.

'She was also temperamental and difficult.'

Looking slightly mollified by that, Nicky sat back. 'So what went wrong?'

Suddenly feeling as if he were sitting on knives, Rafael shifted uncomfortably in his chair. 'Hasn't Gaby told you?'

'No. She's loyal and I didn't like to ask.'

'Let's just say it didn't work out.'

'Yes, the divorce part of it kind of gives that away.'

He shrugged. 'There you go, then.'

Nicky fell silent and for a moment Rafael thought with blessed relief that was that. That she'd understood that he didn't want to talk about it, and that as far as he was concerned the topic was now closed.

But apparently it wasn't, at least not for her, because she was lifting her sunglasses off her nose and up into her hair and giving him a look that suggested that she didn't think him brushing over it quite so dismissively was on.

'Is that it?' she said, clearly not impressed. 'Is that all I'm getting?'

'Isn't that enough?'

'Not nearly.'

'Tough.' That was all he was prepared to divulge.

Nicky harrumphed and folded her arms over her chest. 'Well, that doesn't seem entirely fair, does it?' she said eventually.

Rafael lifted an eyebrow at her indignation. 'What doesn't?'

'I tell you all about the stuff that happened to me yet you get to avoid talking about what happened to you? I don't think so.'

The urge to tense up was back but he stamped it down and pasted a bland smile to his face. 'But the difference is that you *chose* to tell me. Willingly. And I don't particularly like talking about my marriage.'

'I'm sure you don't,' she said archly, 'but you might find it surprisingly therapeutic. I did, after all.'

'I don't need therapy. I got over it years ago.'

She fixed him with another far too perceptive look. 'Really?' she asked with a scepticism that made him want to grind his teeth.

'Absolutely.'

'In that case, why the reluctance to talk about it? And why do you still have such a thing about getting involved with your sisters' friends?'

This time Rafael couldn't stop his jaw from clenching because as he contemplated her irritatingly shrewd questions he realised she had a point. And he, therefore, didn't have much of a choice if he didn't want her thinking she was right. 'Fine,' he said as if it didn't bother him in the slightest. 'What do you want to know?'

Rafael's marriage might have been occupying her mind a lot lately, but Nicky had never had any intention of actually bringing it up.

However she'd been gazing in the direction of the

wedding-goers gathering in front of the church on the other side of the square and idly wondering whether he and the beautiful but temperamental Marina had been married here or in Madrid and what the dress had looked like, when the warmth and the wine and a sheer sense of contentment had obliterated her inhibitions and the question had simply spilled out of her mouth.

Once it had there'd been little point in hoping he hadn't heard her and even less in trying to back-pedal. And if she was being completely honest, she wouldn't have retracted it even if she could because the curiosity had been practically killing her.

She wanted to know everything, and now, thank *God*, it seemed she'd have to wonder and speculate and imagine no longer. 'Why don't you start at the beginning?' she said.

Rafael set his jaw and looked as if he were bracing himself. 'I met Marina through my younger sister.'

'Gaby?'

'The next one up. Elena. She and Marina were best friends. Elena had a party to celebrate her birthday and we were introduced. We dated and three months later we got married.'

Nicky nearly fell off her chair because that didn't sound like the action of the keen-on-control Rafael she'd come to know. 'Wow, that was quick.'

'Too quick with hindsight,' he said dryly.

'How long were you married for?'

'A couple of years.'

'What happened?'

He grimaced. 'Once the honeymoon was over—literally—it became pretty clear that we had nothing in common.'

Nothing? She couldn't believe that. Not when, as she'd discovered, he was intelligent and interesting and had well-formed opinions on an impressively wide range of subjects.

'You must have had *something* in common,' she said, 'otherwise why get married in the first place?'

He rubbed a hand along his jaw and nodded briefly. 'OK, there was one thing,' he conceded and as a pang of jealousy darted through her Nicky wished she hadn't pressed the point. 'But naturally it wasn't enough. We were too different. And too young.'

'How old were you?' she asked, dismissing the jealously as entirely normal and ignoring it.

'I was twenty-three and Marina was twenty.'

'Didn't anyone try and stop you?'

'Of course, but you know how I feel about advice. I'm as bad at taking it as I am at giving it.' He gave her a tight humourless smile. 'Besides, I'd just got back from Harvard and, having had the best education on offer, I thought I knew everything.'

'But you didn't.'

'Apparently not. I certainly knew nothing about how to handle the mess we'd got ourselves into. We argued. A lot. In fact,' he added with a frown, 'we argued about pretty much everything.'

'That sounds stressful.'

'It was.' He stopped and for a moment he seemed to be completely lost in the memory of it all before giving his head a quick shake and snapping out of it. 'Anyway, things went rapidly downhill until I ended up virtually living at the office and Marina ended up having an affair.'

Nicky winced. 'Ouch.'

Rafael sighed. 'I can't say I really blame her. We should never have got married in the first place. The whole thing was a disaster from start to finish and it's not something I'm in a hurry to do again.'

At the thought of him, normally so focused and so in control, so way out of his depth and floundering in the face of such unfathomably emotional upheaval, Nicky felt her heart squeeze. 'So how did your sister take it all?'

He went very still and a muscle ticced in his jaw. 'It wasn't the easiest of times,' he muttered eventually. 'We didn't see all that much of each other for a while. It was…awkward.'

'Just awkward?' she asked, thinking that for someone who clearly adored his sisters—even if they did occasionally drive him up the wall—'awkward' was more likely to mean 'gut-wrenching'.

'OK, yes, it was more than awkward,' he admitted, 'but you know all about the healing powers of time.'

She nodded. 'I do indeed.'

'We got through it eventually but that isn't something I'd care to repeat either.'

No, she could see why he wouldn't want to repeat any of it. And she could equally see why he went to such great lengths to avoid emotional mess now because she'd do the same in the circumstances. Who needed it?

Feeling faintly guilty at having made him relive what had clearly been a difficult time, Nicky decided the situation needed lightening.

'It's just as well I'm not blonde, beautiful, temperamental or difficult, then, isn't it?' she said, flashing him a teasing smile.

Rafael stared at her, bewilderment flickering across his face. 'What?'

'Well, when this is over we should be able to part as friends, don't you think? I certainly don't intend to lose Gaby's friendship over it.'

For a moment there was utter silence and Nicky wondered what she'd said. Then Rafael seemed to pull himself together and shot her a quick stomach-melting smile. 'This is quite different,' he said, and signalled for the bill.

* * *

It *was* different, thought Rafael, shoving his hands in the pockets of his jeans and leaning back against a low wall as he watched Nicky hunker down at the bottom of some steps and lift her camera to her eye.

And thank God for it because his relationship with Marina had been a disaster. A complete disaster, and not just because they'd been young and had had precious little in common. Yes, those had obviously been contributing factors to the breakdown of their marriage, but what had really been at the heart of it all was Marina's clinginess and neediness and his inability to handle any of it.

With hindsight he should have foreseen problems right from the start, or at least the minute he'd learned about her overprotective parents, the sheltered life she'd led and her desperate longing to escape.

If he'd been thinking straight he'd have paid attention to the great neon warnings his brain kept flashing at him and steered well clear, but in all honesty they'd met and he'd been so dazzled by her looks he'd stopped thinking at all.

It hadn't helped that meeting her had coincided with his return to Spain after years of hard academic work and little play. He'd been demob happy and hell-bent on making up for lost time and she'd been only too willing to help. So he hadn't stopped to think about what effect their whirlwind romance might have had on her and it had never occurred to him that she'd start to view him as some sort of saviour.

But she had, and before long the signs of her dependency on him had become apparent. She'd turned possessive, jealous and obsessive, calling him a dozen times a day just to check where he was and what he was doing. She'd stopped seeing the few friends she had and tried to stop him seeing the friends he had.

He'd unwittingly found himself responsible for her happiness and he hadn't known what to do. And then it had got even worse because by the time he realised how needy and stifling she'd become—and how unhappy he made her— he'd also realised that he'd confused lust with love and that by marrying her he'd made a massive mistake.

And the awful guilt-inducing truth of the matter was that he hadn't even thought about trying to sort things out, trying to make it work, because ultimately he hadn't cared. Not during their fiercest arguments, not when Marina had had the affair and not even when she'd filed for divorce.

In fact the bureaucratic nightmare of the divorce had given him a greater headache than his marriage had, and the distress it had caused his sister, who'd been torn between her brother and her best friend, had given him greater heartache.

Which was so wholly *wrong* he'd vowed never to let himself get into that kind of a situation again. Never again was he going to mistake lust for love, thought Rafael, narrowing his eyes and setting his jaw as he watched Nicky, who was totally absorbed in what she was doing. Nor did he intend to ever get himself into a relationship where he might find himself depended on. For anything. The responsibility of it all was simply too great and he'd only screw up. Again.

And that was why being with Nicky was so refreshing. He admired the way she kept her cards close to her chest, had the ability to sort things through in her own head and didn't ask anything of him. Above all he appreciated the way he could be himself, the way he didn't feel he had to be constantly on his guard in case she wanted more than he was able to give, because she never would.

The thought of pursuing a more long-term relationship with her popped up in his head once again and his muscles tensed and his heart beat a fraction faster as the need to get started on it right now surged up inside him.

What was the point in waiting? In deliberating? There

wasn't any, was there? Because it seemed to him that she was just as into this as he was, and he didn't think she'd say no. At least he fervently hoped she wouldn't.

Rafael was just about to push himself off the wall and head towards her when he saw her shoot to her feet, take a quick step back and crash straight into a group of tourists who'd gathered behind her and were listening to the guide gesticulating at the memorial she'd been photographing.

If he'd had time to think about it—and if it had been anyone else other than Nicky—he'd have expected her to brush herself off, give them a quick smile and a heartfelt apology and then stroll back to him.

But he didn't have time to think because it all happened so fast. So fast in fact that his brain slowed it right down.

He watched as Nicky froze and went white and then stumbled, and within what felt like aeons but could only have been a split second the little group was closing round her, hands reaching out to steady her.

As alarm began to flash through him he heard her cry of distress. Saw her lash out, and as he realised what was going on he didn't stop to think or consider his actions. He just reacted.

With his heart pounding as fiercely as he bet hers was and with adrenalin suddenly roaring through him, he raced over. Muttering a rough apology, he pushed his way through the crowd to where Nicky was standing, pale, sweating and shaking. He wrapped one arm around her waist, the other around her shoulders and drew her into a firm embrace.

'It's all right. You're OK,' he murmured against her hair, every cell of his body turning inside out with the need to absorb her panic and give her some of his strength. 'Lean on me. I've got you.'

CHAPTER THIRTEEN

I'VE GOT YOU.

As Rafael tightened his grip on Nicky's waist and led her away from the group of people and their curiosity at her extraordinary reaction to their mini collision, the words he was murmuring into her hair over and over spun round and round her head because now all the panic and confusion had evaporated it suddenly struck her that he *did* get her. He really did.

There she'd been a moment ago, surrounded and trapped and in the terrifying grip of a flashback, her heart hammering and panic drowning out the voice of common sense that was telling her the hands on her were only trying to steady her and that she wasn't in any danger. And then, just when her knees had been about to give way, just when she'd thought she'd been about to faint and almost falling apart at the awareness that she *still* wasn't as over everything as she'd thought, there *he'd* been, charging to her rescue like some kind of white knight, taking her into his arms and shielding her from the nightmare, warm and solid and so very reassuring.

She hadn't had to ask for his help. She hadn't had to spell it out. He'd somehow instinctively known what was wrong, and he'd put it right.

He'd got it.

He got *her*.

And not only a second ago, she thought dazedly as Rafael leaned back against the wall of the church and held her tight still murmuring soothing words into her hair. The truth of it was that over the last week he'd often appeared to be able to read her mind, apparently understanding exactly what she needed—whether it was space, silence or company—sometimes even before she did. And she'd been able to gauge his moods too.

It was as if they had some kind of connection and the weird thing was that, far from finding it unsettling as she should have done, she'd actually revelled in it. Which meant that not only did he get her, but that she *wanted* him to.

As *that* thought slammed into her head Nicky's slowing heart began to race all over again because hot on the heels of it came a whole load more, cascading into her head so fast that she went dizzy.

Oh, dear Lord. The attention and care he'd lavished on her in the last few days? She loved it. The feeling of being cherished, protected, looked after? She loved all that too. And as for the way he'd just rushed to her rescue, well, that melted just about every independent feminist thought she'd ever had.

She ought to have found it stifling, but she didn't. She ought to have been horrified that it went against everything she'd ever thought she'd valued, but she found she couldn't drum up much objection to that either.

And why not?

Because she was head over heels bonkers in love with him.

Nicky froze, her pulse going berserk and her knees threatening to buckle all over again.

She was in love with him. She had to be. What else could account for it all?

She'd never really thought about falling in love. Never

imagined she would. Never expected it. It wasn't that she didn't believe in it as a concept, and it wasn't as if she hadn't had a good example of it set by her parents. It was just that she'd never felt it herself before. She'd always been too busy to look for it. Too focused on staying on the move and remaining unattached.

But not any more because now she was thinking about it she was beginning to realise that she loved everything about him. And it had nothing whatsoever to do with the mind-blowing sex, because even when they weren't in bed she still had that wonderfully warm sense of contentment. Every time he smiled at her, every time he looked at her and every time he touched her. In fact every time he crossed her mind her heart turned over and she went soft and warm inside.

If that wasn't love, then what was it?

And just like that all those things that had been baffling her recently suddenly made sense. Her lack of enthusiasm about going back to Paris. The longing to learn everything there was to know about him. The brief jagged pain that scythed through her at the thought of them being over. The wrenching of her heart when she'd caught sight of the couple floating out of the church not five minutes ago, beaming and radiating happiness and wrapped round each other as they posed for photographs beneath a Mudéjar arch. And the couple of dark-haired green-eyed children she'd secretly imagined racing around the *cortijo*...

As her muscles gently collapsed beneath the deluge of emotion descending over her Nicky sank against him. God. Not a fan of emotional mess? Who had she been kidding? She'd never wanted it more. She wanted the roller coaster of the ride. The highs and the lows, the laughter and the arguments. She was bone-deep tired of being footloose and fancy free, of the endless travel and being alone. She wanted to settle down. She wanted someone to share her life with. She wanted Rafael.

Her heart thumped as her mind raced. But what about him? How did he feel about her? Could she even begin to hope he might love her back? Yes, she'd noticed his concern for her, the way he'd cared for her, the warmth with which he looked at her, but did any of that mean anything? Surely it had to mean *something*…

Listening to the steady beat of his heart beneath her cheek and taking strength from the arms around her and the warm hard body still supporting her, she sifted through all the evidence, analysing every look and every smile he'd given her, every little thing he'd said and done, and her heart thumped wildly as she came to the conclusion that he very well could.

And OK, from what she'd just learned about his marriage of course he'd be wary of loving again and wary of commitment, but maybe she could show him that with someone who understood him, with *her*, he needn't be.

Nicky closed her eyes and took a deep breath, inhaling the intoxicating scent of him as she struggled to absorb all these earth-shattering discoveries and would have swayed had she not been locked in his embrace.

'Would you like to go home?' he said softly.

And just when she thought her system couldn't cope with any more shocks, wham, there was another one, because didn't *home* sound like the most heavenly thing ever?

She'd never had a home before. Never wanted one. If she'd ever thought about it she'd have shuddered at the idea of anything so permanent. So cosy. So boringly domestic. But that long-held belief went the way of the others and exploded into smithereens because right now she couldn't think of anywhere she'd rather be than with Rafael. At home. For ever.

Feeling that the world had somehow tilted violently and

then settled back down all upside down, Nicky dazedly leaned back in his arms, smiled up into his eyes and said, 'Yes, please.'

The fact that Nicky didn't seem to have anything to say during the car journey back to the *cortijo* suited Rafael down to the ground because there was so much stuff churning around in his head he didn't think he'd be able to hold anything remotely resembling a conversation even if she'd wanted one.

At some point between taking her in his arms to lead her to safety and getting in the car something had changed. What precisely it was he couldn't work out. All he knew was that something was different, it was deeply unsettling and for some reason it threw his idea of a long-term relationship with Nicky right on its head.

He'd been leaning back against that wall and holding her close when he'd felt her stiffen, then soften. All of a sudden it had seemed to him that she was pressing just that little bit closer and not because she wanted to get horizontal and naked with him but because she wanted to simply be with him.

For some reason the idea of it had made him reel. It had made him prickle with foreboding and fill with trepidation. And then, before he'd had time to recover and to reassure himself that he was merely still shaken up by what he'd seen Nicky just go through and must have imagined it, she'd smiled up at him, her eyes shining and her face all soft and dreamy. She'd looked at him as if he were her knight in shining armour and his heart had given a sudden lurch because at that moment tough, resilient, independent Nicky had been replaced by someone he didn't recognise.

And frankly it spooked the hell out of him.

'Rafael, are you all right?'

His hands tightened on the steering wheel and he wished they were home already so he could put some distance between them. 'Fine,' he muttered. 'Why?'

'You're very quiet.'

'Just thinking, that's all.'

'About what happened back there?'

'Partly.'

'Me too.' There it was again, that dreamy wistfulness in her voice drifting through the dark, winding through him and twisting his gut into knots. 'Thank you for coming to my rescue.'

Rafael tensed and felt a bead of sweat trickle down his spine as his stomach instinctively clutched tighter. 'You're welcome.'

'I'll have to make sure you're around every time I find myself unexpectedly in the middle of a crowd.'

Her words hit his brain and Rafael went utterly cold, because despite the faint teasing note in her voice he didn't think she was joking. And if she wasn't joking, then he was in a whole lot of trouble. And if he was, then it was all entirely of his own making.

The knowledge struck him like a blow and he inhaled sharply. God, he'd been a fool. He'd told Nicky to lean on him and that was precisely what she'd done. And not, he could now see, in a solely literal sense. Nor only back in that square. She'd been leaning on him ever since he'd brought her back down here and like a blind idiot he hadn't seen it.

In fact he'd been *provoking* it.

He'd thought he'd simply been keeping an eye on her. Making sure she was OK. Spending time with her, getting to know her and encouraging her to talk about what had happened in the Middle East to help her get over it. But what he'd really been doing over the course of the last week was creating an environment in which she was *bound* to come to depend on him.

How he could have forgotten that she might not be as fully recovered as she claimed he had no idea. Hadn't she woken up in the early hours, sweating and trembling, only a couple of nights ago? She had, and without a thought for the consequences he'd gathered her in his arms and held her until she'd stopped shaking with fear and started quivering with something else entirely.

And then back there in the square he'd rushed to her side, and that must have fanned the flames because, God, the way she'd smiled up at him... As if he'd rescued her from more than just a flashback...

Rafael's blood chilled. He wasn't that man. He couldn't be. He couldn't be responsible for her well-being because he'd only fail and very probably set her back months.

So he could forget any idea of a long-distance, more permanent relationship, he thought with grim resolve. Things had already gone far too far and the minute they got back to the *cortijo* he'd be putting a stop to this affair, this budding relationship, this whatever it was, once and for all.

'Rafael?'

'What?' he growled, completely lost in thought.

'I think I love you.'

Perhaps Rafael's car in the dead of night wasn't the best place to blurt out she loved him, thought Nicky, clinging onto the door handle as the car swerved briefly before being hauled back under control, but really she hadn't had much of a choice. She'd never been one to tackle things anything other than head-on, so once she'd realised she loved him and wanted something more with him the need to spill it out had bubbled and built until it just sort of erupted from her.

But maybe she should have told him while they were in

bed or something because she didn't know what reaction she'd been expecting but she'd known what she'd been hoping for, and the short sharp curse, the fierce scowl, and the crackling tension that was suddenly filling the space between them wasn't it.

But it was way too late for regret. Her declaration was out there, the words were echoing between them in the thick darkness and there was no taking it back. All she could do now was brace herself for his response.

Releasing her death grip on the door handle, Nicky swivelled slightly to look at him and, with her heart in her throat, waited.

And waited.

And waited.

But to her growing bewilderment Rafael remained resolutely silent, his jaw tight and his focus fixed on the road ahead, and with every kilometre that the car gobbled up she went a little colder.

'Aren't you going to say anything?' she asked, when the deafening silence finally became unbearable.

'What do you want me to say?'

At the complete lack of emotion in his voice it dawned on her that this conversation was unlikely to go the way she'd have liked, and Nicky filled with apprehension. 'I don't know,' she said, suddenly feeling all shaky inside. 'How about thank you? I'm flattered. I love you too. *Something*.'

'I'm sorry,' he said flatly, 'but you don't love me.'

For a moment she thought she must have misheard, but no, he really had just told her that she didn't love him.

As it sank in Nicky felt her eyes widen and her jaw drop because of all the responses she could have imagined an outright denial of her feelings would never have occurred to her. 'What?' she breathed.

'You don't love me. You just think you do.' He shot her

a quick unfathomable look. 'I'm not some kind of white knight, Nicky.'

She blinked. 'I know you're not.'

'Do you?' His jaw tightened.

'Of course.' She might have had a moment of fancy back there in the square but that was all it had been because she knew perfectly well that, not only did Rafael have feet of clay like everyone else, but she didn't need a knight.

'I can't be responsible for your well-being.'

Confusion spun through her. Had she missed something? Had they had a conversation she'd forgotten about? They must have done because where was all this coming from? How on earth had they got from her telling him she loved him to this? And where had this God complex suddenly sprung from? 'What makes you think you are?'

'Your comment about needing me around whenever you find yourself in a crowd.'

'That was a *joke*.'

'It didn't sound like one.'

And maybe it hadn't been one *totally*, but that wasn't the point. 'I see,' she said, folding her arms over her chest and feeling her blood beginning to simmer in response to his baffling attitude. 'And you've deduced from that that I've somehow cast you in the role of knight in shining armour?'

'Haven't you?'

'Of course not.'

'It wouldn't be your fault if you had.' His face tightened. 'This last week has been a mistake,' he muttered, almost as if talking to himself. '*My* mistake.'

Did he really believe that? The hurt that suddenly cut through her momentarily robbed her of breath. 'Why?'

'Because I've let you become dependent on me and I shouldn't have.'

She let out a slow measured breath to stop the top of her

head blowing off. 'You know, your arrogance is truly stag-gering,' she said, staring at him in stupefaction as all the lovely warmth and the dizzying sense of wonder that had been bubbling away inside her for the last hour or so evap-orated.

Rafael whipped his head round to give her a quick glance and she saw astonishment written all over his face. 'What?'

'I'm perfectly capable of being responsible for my own well-being,' she said, silently adding, *You jerk*. 'Like it or not, I'm in love with you.' Although right now she really wished she weren't. 'And it has nothing to do with my re-covery or dependency or whatever you think you've been doing over the last week.'

'You can't be,' he said flatly. 'We haven't known each other long enough. You're confusing love and lust, that's all.'

Nicky fought not to gape at him as her head spun. What the hell was going on here? Who was this? Where was the Rafael she'd fallen in love with? The warm, thoughtful man who'd made her laugh and who'd made such passionate love to her. The one she'd got to know and admire. He had to still be there somewhere but why had he switched himself off like this?

And then suddenly a great wave of hurt and disappoint-ment swept through her, boiling her blood and firing her in-dignation. If he didn't feel the same way about her as she did about him that was fine. Painful, but fair enough. But this casual and cold dismissal of her feelings? No, that wasn't right and it wasn't fair.

'How dare you?' she breathed.

'What?' he said, casting her a quick cool glance as if he genuinely didn't have a clue what she meant.

'How dare you just brush me off like that?'

He shrugged. 'Because I know what I'm talking about.' The condescension in his voice made her want to slap him.

'It happened to me. In my marriage. I thought I married for love. It turned out to be nothing more than lust.'

'And you think that's what's going on here?'

'If it's not dependency, then very possibly. Have you ever been in love before?'

'Well, no, but—'

'Then how do you know that what you claim to feel for me isn't love, but simply lust?'

And once again he rendered her speechless. She just sat there, totally bamboozled by his logic and unable to breathe. She felt winded, as if he'd struck her square in the chest.

And then sensation came flooding back, and all that hurt and disappointment and frustration at his reaction now combined with dizzying and unfamiliar red hot anger, and the whole lot of it surged through her in one great unstoppable wave.

'I'll tell you how I know,' she said, feeling what little control she had when it came to him slipping away but too consumed by all the emotions tossing around inside her to do anything about it. 'I know because even if we never made love again I'd still want to be with you. I know because I admire you and respect you and because I think you're amazing. Yes, I love the way you make me feel, but it's so much more than that.' She glared at him. 'And you know how I *really* know it's love and not lust?'

'How?' he said, sounding as if he couldn't be less interested.

'By the way that your casual dismissal of what I feel is practically crucifying me.'

Rafael went still, but he didn't look at her. 'If I've hurt you, then I apologise, but perhaps it's for the best.'

'For the best?' she echoed.

'Better now than months down the line.'

God, she really had got it wrong, hadn't she? Terribly,

agonisingly wrong. 'Are you honestly saying that you feel nothing for me?'

Rafael frowned. 'I wouldn't say nothing. I like you a lot and I can't get enough of you in bed. But as I said, that's just lust.'

'And what about if sex wasn't part of the equation?'

'I would rapidly lose interest.'

His voice might be flat and cold but the muscle ticcing madly in his jaw suggested he wasn't as unaffected as he was trying to make out, and suddenly a tiny ray of hope burst through the tangle of hurt and confusion and anger within her. 'I don't believe you.'

He shrugged. 'That's up to you.'

As all the things he'd done for her, the way he'd held her, made love to her, talked to her flashed through her head she took a deep breath and a massive gamble. 'I think you love me too.'

'You couldn't be more wrong, because I don't.'

She let out that breath in a furious exasperated rush, suddenly utterly fed up with him. 'God, I've never met such a stubborn, thick-headed man in my life. Nor one who is such an emotional coward.'

That jerked him out of his indifference. He snapped his gaze to hers, his eyes blazing. *'What?'*

Nicky gripped her seat belt and refused to quail. 'You're an emotional coward, Rafael.'

He snapped his gaze back to the road. 'What the hell do you mean by that?'

'Every time the going gets tough, every time something crops up that you don't want to deal with, you retreat.'

'I do not.'

'No?' she said. 'OK, well, let's take a look at the evidence.'

'Don't be ridiculous. There is no evidence.'

'You think?' She held up her hand and ticked off her index

finger. 'Firstly there's your marriage. Things started getting difficult and you buried yourself in your work.'

'Don't even begin to presume you know what went on in my marriage,' he said icily calmly.

Nicky ignored his chilling fury. 'I wouldn't dream of it. But you even admitted that much, once you managed to get past your reluctance to talk about it in the first place. And then what about that time we met?' She wiggled her middle finger.

'What about it?'

'Weren't you escaping from the demands of two sisters, one mother and an ex-girlfriend?'

He gritted his teeth and his eyes flashed her a warning but she wasn't about to stop now. 'And then there was that kiss by the pool,' she fired at him, giving up with the fingers altogether. 'You might not have physically fled then, but emotionally you did, and you're doing it again now. Going straight into denial and retreating, just because I'm being honest and you can't deal with it. You look like you're itching to escape and the only reason you're not is because we're in your car flying along at seventy kilometres an hour and you can't.' She gave him a withering look. 'And you know something—while kind of understandable in a boy of eight, in a man of thirty-two it's pathetic.'

Her words hung in the air, suspended between them, the seconds ticking heavily by before he said, 'Yes, well, we can't all be wild, adventurous risk-takers like you.'

She stared at him. 'You see being honest and dealing with emotions as a risk?'

'Absolutely.'

'Then what about the rewards?'

'In my experience there aren't any.'

Ooh, she wanted to thump him. 'If you truly think that, then that's sad. Yes, I take risks—' and none more so than the one she'd taken just now '—but they're generally calculated ones. And even if one does go wrong—' as this one seemed to be doing '—at least I tried. But what do you do? You hide.'

'It's called self-preservation.'

'It's called immaturity.'

Rafael flinched as if she'd struck him, but Nicky hadn't finished. They might have arrived back at the *cortijo* and he might be yanking on the handbrake and reaching for the clip of his seat belt as if he couldn't get away fast enough, but she matched him for speed. 'You think you're so good at solving problems and sorting out things for other people,' she said, freeing herself and reaching for the door, 'but what about you? Who sorts you out?' She glared at him. 'Right now the biggest problem here is you and your absurd refusal to even entertain the thought about how you might feel about me, and you're not even bothering to try and fix it even though you could.'

'There's nothing to fix.'

'There could be.'

'There won't be.'

He got out of the car and slammed the door shut, and it finally hit her that she'd never be able to get through to him. That he'd been hiding his emotions away for too long and too well. Nothing she could say or do would ever have any effect on him and Nicky had suddenly had enough.

'Well, if that really is the case,' she said, her voice shaking with anger, 'then this time *I'm* the one walking away.'

Nicky was wrong, thought Rafael grimly as the slam of the front door reverberated throughout the *cortijo*, leaving nothing but an eerie silence and the echo of all those accusations.

Dead wrong. About everything.

As if he needed sorting out. As if he needed fixing. The

idea was laughable. He didn't need either. He was fine the way he was.

And if he did occasionally retreat, well, what was the problem with that? As he'd told her, it was simply a question of self-preservation, that was all. It worked for his father and it worked for him. He had it under control. It wasn't an issue. And it wasn't immaturity. And what would she know about it anyway? She didn't have a vast family that constantly badgered her, did she?

And OK, he might have been a bit thrown by that conversation about Marina and all the memories it had tossed up, and he might possibly have got it wrong about her being dependent on him, but as for them being in love with each other, well, that was completely absurd.

He wasn't in love with her and she wasn't in love with him. She couldn't be. They'd only known each other for a few weeks. It wasn't possible.

So it was a good thing she'd gone, wasn't it, because, God, all that emotion… It had been horrible…

Stifling a shudder, Rafael stalked into the drawing room and strode towards the drinks cabinet. He reached for the brandy and filled a glass and winced as all the things Nicky had said and the way she'd said them hit him all over again. He tossed his drink back in one and hoped the burning alcohol that hit his stomach would obliterate the memory of the last half an hour.

At least it was all over now, which was excellent because he didn't need this kind of hassle in his life. He didn't need this kind of upheaval. And he could certainly do without feeling like this.

Whatever it was that was coursing through him right now it couldn't possibly be something serious like hurt or disappointment or regret or anything. It was simply shock at the abruptness of her departure, that was all. And if he did feel a tiny pang of loss, well, that was only natural given the intensity and passion that their affair had had.

Like everything, recovering from it would simply be a question of patience and time, and with a bit of both he'd soon come to appreciate the lucky escape he'd had.

CHAPTER FOURTEEN

NICKY'S ANGER SUSTAINED her throughout the entire horren-
dous journey back to Paris. She bristled and fumed her way
through the tiresome process of handing back her hire car,
the booking of a last-minute, excruciatingly expensive flight,
and, what with a three hour delay and a diversion to Orly,
staying furious hadn't taken all that much effort.

The teeth-grinding frustration of international travel not-
withstanding, all she had to do was remember how she'd laid
her heart, her feelings, everything she had on the line and
how Rafael had trampled all over them, and it rose up inside
her all over again. She'd mentally called him every filthy
name she could think of in both English and French, and told
herself over and over again that she was well shot of him.

But the minute she closed her front door behind her the
adrenalin and energy drained right away sweeping up all her
anger and strength with it, and with a low anguished moan
she crumpled into a heap on the floor.

As despair and misery filled the gaping hole left inside
her, she finally gave in to the wretchedness and tears spilled
down her cheeks because she might be well shot of him but
she was still crazy about him. Her heart felt as if it were
being wrenched from her chest. Her head pounded, her throat
burned and she ached all over.

Oh, how could it all hurt so *much*? And why was she crying like this? She never cried. Now, though, it seemed she couldn't stop.

Burying her head in her hands as yet more tears welled up, Nicky reran the whole horrible conversation and with her anger at Rafael's reaction all burned out she now helplessly charged off down the road of self-recrimination.

Why, oh, why had she had to say anything? Why had she had to go and tell him she loved him? Why couldn't she just have kept it to herself?

She wrapped her arms around herself and rocked as re-gret spun through her. How could she have let rip at him like that? What gave her the right to fire all that stuff about his issues at him? And as for telling him he loved her, well, who the hell was she to assume that that was the case? He'd never given her that impression, had he? No, her common sense had been shot to pieces by everything that had hap-pened in the previous half an hour and she'd jumped to that ridiculous conclusion all by herself.

She'd lost all control and because of it she'd never see him again. Her throat ached and her eyes stung all over again and she let out a quiet anguished moan as what little was left of her heart shattered.

God, if this was love then she was lucky to have escaped it for the past twenty-nine years because she'd never known agony like it. Never felt hopelessness like it, not even when she'd been at rock-bottom.

How long she sat there, crying and tormenting herself with what ifs and if onlys, she had no idea. All she knew was that by the time she was all wrung out and had no tears left, long silvery grey fingers of daylight were inching through the slats in her blinds.

With a deep sigh, Nicky wiped her eyes with the sleeve of her coat, sniffed unattractively and pulled herself together. This wasn't doing her any good, was it? She might be feeling battered and bruised but she couldn't stay here wallowing in self-pity for ever.

Groggily she got to her feet. She swayed a little and had to lean against the wall for support. Her limbs felt like jelly and she hurt everywhere but she gritted her teeth and made it into the kitchen because maybe things would look a bit brighter after coffee.

There was something remarkably restful about going through the motions of filling the pot with water, adding the coffee grounds to the filter and then screwing the top on. Something comfortably familiar, and as she put the pot on the hob, lit the gas and then leaned back against the counter to let it do its thing she determinedly rallied her spirits.

She might have screwed up whatever she and Rafael had had by recklessly telling him she loved him, but one good thing had come out of that whole mess of a conversation, and that was that she'd been right about wanting to settle down.

Despite the considerable progress she'd made she still—frustratingly—wasn't one hundred per cent back to her old self, so maybe she did need a bit of permanency to give herself the chance and time to focus on her.

And she might not have Rafael to settle down with but that didn't mean she couldn't do it anyway, did it?

Of course she could. She might love him, but she didn't *need* him. Even before she'd realised she loved him, she'd been toying with the idea of making changes to her life, and she was perfectly capable of making those changes on her own. In fact with no one else to consult, with no one to offer an opinion and advice, it would probably be easier.

She'd start now, she thought, pouring a cup of coffee and taking a hot fortifying sip. Thinking positively was the thing. Staying buoyant and remaining focused. And in the process she was bound to forget all about him.

* * *

This was getting ridiculous.

Rafael was sitting at his desk again, ignoring the files piled up in front of him again and staring blankly into space. Again.

With a growl of frustration he pushed his chair back, stalked over to the window and scowled down at the city spreading far below. What the hell *was* this? Why couldn't he focus? And where had this incessant restlessness and edginess come from?

He'd been back in Madrid for a week now, and every single minute of it had been diabolically awful.

He should have been fine. God knew he had plenty to occupy himself. The new job he'd taken on—sorting out a company whose management structure was so top heavy that it was in danger of toppling over—gave him enough work to keep him busy for months. But to his intense irritation he wasn't fine.

He couldn't concentrate on anything. He couldn't eat, couldn't sleep, and it was driving him nuts. He was cross, tired, hungry and frustrated, which, as he never usually got cross, tired, hungry or frustrated, only made it all ten times worse.

He should have been thinking about ways to flatten out his client's absurdly rigid management hierarchy. He should have been drawing up proposals and schedules and setting up meetings, but was he? No. All he could think about was that if ending things with Nicky had been for the best why wasn't he rejoicing at having had such a remarkably lucky escape? Why did her accusations keep ricocheting around his head as if on some bloody unstoppable loop? And why hadn't that stab of loss gone away?

He'd had plenty of time to forget her and he'd used up practically every drop of his patience trying to do just that, but neither had made a blind bit of difference because he simply couldn't get her out of his head. She was in there all the damn time, sometimes distracting him with her smiles, her voice and that maddening habit she had of biting on her lip whenever she was thinking, but more often sitting in the darkness of his car, spitting fury and flinging all those awful things at him.

For the life of him he couldn't work out why what she'd said was having such an effect on him. It wasn't as if he'd sat around deliberately dwelling on it. No. In fact he'd never been busier. Apart from the welcome distraction of work, he'd taken his mother out to a hip new restaurant. He'd caught up with Gaby. And yesterday he'd spotted a new bud on the baobab he'd grown from seed.

But the food in that restaurant had tasted like cardboard. All he'd wanted to ask Gaby was if she'd seen Nicky, and the new baobab bud left him oddly numb.

None of his usual fail-safe methods of self-preservation had worked and he'd now got to the stage he wished he could reach down, yank out everything that was churning around inside him and twisting him into knots and toss it in the bin because it was all driving him insane.

Especially the guilt that at some point over the last week had taken up what was turning out to be permanent residence in his conscience. The guilt that, along with the little voice that had been niggling away in his head, was beginning to suggest that firstly he'd behaved appallingly and that secondly Nicky might have had a point.

For days he'd tried to resist both. For days he'd been telling himself that his reaction to her declaration she was in love with him had been perfectly normal given his experience with Marina, and that of course Nicky hadn't had a point.

But right now he was just so *tired*. And not just physically. He was tired of resisting. Tired of constantly lying to himself—or at the very least denying the truth—and tired of trying to forget her.

Rafael rubbed a hand over his face as for what felt like the billionth time everything she'd said, everything she'd accused him of, ran through his head. And as something deep inside him finally gave way, fracturing and crumbling into dust, the truth smacked him right between the eyes.

Nicky had been deadly accurate in summing him up, hadn't she? He *did* back off and run when the going got tough. He'd started the moment he'd decided he'd had enough of his sisters hassling him when he'd been a boy and escaped to the end of the garden, and he'd never stopped. He'd done it with Marina, he'd done it with his sisters and his mother and his girlfriends and he'd done it with Nicky. Every time, every single time he faced anything that might require an emotional response he fought to escape. And if he couldn't he shut himself down.

Look at what had happened when Nicky had told him she loved him. He'd been cold. Dismissive. Cruel. He'd hurt her. Crucified her, she'd said. And why? Because he'd been unable to handle it. Unable to let himself believe it, because if he allowed himself to believe it then what else might he end up believing?

Rafael stumbled over to his chair just in time to sink into it and buried his head in his hands as the now unfettered truth rained down on him.

God, he *was* the problem, wasn't he? She'd accused him of being pathetic, stubborn and thick-headed, and he was, because was he *really* still hung up on what had happened with his marriage? It was nearly ten years ago, for heaven's sake. He wasn't twenty-three and Nicky wasn't Marina.

She wasn't needy and clingy and desperate for his attention, and of *course* she didn't depend on him for her recovery or her well-being or anything else. She'd been taking care of herself for years.

And he *did* know the difference between lust and love, didn't he?

Taking a deep breath, Rafael made himself face up to the facts he'd stupidly and lily-liveredly shied away from in an absurd effort to distance himself from Nicky and the way she made him feel, his pulse racing and his breathing shallowing.

It wasn't lust that had made him wish he'd been there to protect her when she'd been attacked on that assignment. It wasn't lust that had made him want to look after her that week at the *cortijo*. And it certainly wasn't lust that was making his heart ache like this.

It was love.

And how else did he know? He knew because when she smiled his world brightened. When she looked at him his stomach melted. During the last seven days it hadn't just been the sex he'd missed, but the very essence of her. He'd missed her laugh, her teasing and her vibrancy.

And he knew because for the first time in his life he wanted everything he thought he feared. He wanted to be someone she could depend on. Someone she could turn to for advice and support and comfort.

As wave after wave of emotion swept through him Rafael's hands shook with the force of it.

God, he loved everything about her. She was the bravest, most incredible woman he'd ever met and he'd been a blinkered, idiotic fool. Well, not any more, he thought, suddenly jerking upright and filling with grim determination. Enough was enough and he was through with hiding.

Making a snap decision, he leapt to his feet and scooped up his wallet and his car keys. She wanted honesty and emotion and risk-taking from him? She'd get it.

He could only hope he hadn't left it too late.

CHAPTER FIFTEEN

BUOYANCY, FOCUS AND positive thinking had been pretty hard to maintain when she'd been feeling so up and down but Nicky didn't think she'd done too badly over the last week or so.

For the first few days following her return home she'd swung like some sort of demented pendulum between utter misery at the thought of never seeing Rafael again and the grimly satisfying conviction that she was better off without him. But lately she'd come to terms with the fact that they were well and truly finished and that she was once again on her own, and, while she'd never claim to be happy about it, she had, at least, reached a place where she didn't feel winded whenever she thought about him or about what might have been. Well, not *every* time.

So by and large she reckoned she was making good progress, especially with the changes she'd decided to implement. She'd thrown out her suitcase. Made some calls. Fired off a couple of exploratory emails and bought a few bits and pieces for her flat. When she wasn't thinking about Rafael she felt calm, grounded, and, for the first time in her life, settled.

Any day now she might even be able to delete the photos she'd taken during the time she'd spent at the *cortijo* because while some of them were pretty good she knew perfectly well that that chapter of her life was over and that she needed to move on.

But telling herself to wipe the folder and actually doing it were poles apart, and every time she sat down to click on the 'delete' button she invariably found herself clicking on the 'play slide show' button instead.

Which was precisely what had happened a couple of minutes ago. She'd slid into her chair and opened up the folder, telling herself that she really would do it this time, yet here she was sitting at her desk, staring with longing at the monitor and trying for the billionth time not to think about what might have been if only she'd kept her big mouth shut.

The pictures slowly flipped across the screen and as they did Nicky felt her throat begin to ache all over again. Photo after photo of the grapes, of the vineyards and the people who worked in them, of the arid countryside, and more of Rafael than she'd ever imagined she'd taken flashed before her eyes.

She sighed and her heart squeezed as his gorgeous face filled the screen yet again. In this particular head-shot, he was looking straight at the camera, smiling at her, his eyes a lovely clear green in the bright sunlight, and as she surreptitiously hit 'pause' her mind instantly flew back to the moment she'd taken it. He'd been talking to one of the workers and as if he'd felt her eyes on him had suddenly looked up. Within moments he'd been striding over to her and taking her by the hand and dragging her into the house from where they hadn't emerged till dark.

A wave of melancholy washed over her and Nicky closed her eyes and pinched the bridge of her nose. Swallowing hard, she opened her eyes and set her jaw. She had to get a grip. She really did. She couldn't carry on wafting around like this. Foolishly indulging herself and romanticising everything that had gone on.

She had to do it now. Right now.

Naturally the pain would be sharp but it would be short and final and at *last* she'd be able to move on.

Taking a deep breath and bracing herself, she slid the mouse across her desk so that the cursor was hovering over the 'delete' button and her finger was hovering over the mouse. She dithered. She frowned. She bit her lip. Then she was lifting her chin, clenching her jaw just that little bit more and lowering her forefinger, about to press it and delete the lingering traces of Rafael from her life when the sound of her buzzer ricocheted through her flat and jolted her out of the bubble she'd been in.

No. She wasn't ready, she told herself, her heart thumping as she whipped the mouse up to close the folder instead of deleting it. She really wasn't. Maybe tomorrow…

Shaking her head in despair at her own pathetically weak resolve but reassuring herself that at some point this futile obsession with Rafael had to fade, she jumped up, headed to the kitchen and picked up the handset. 'Hello?'

'Hi,' came the voice from the other end of the intercom and she nearly dropped the handset because she knew of only one voice that deep, that sexy, and only one voice that spread through her like treacle and had the ability to make her shiver with nothing more than a simple 'hi'.

'Rafael?' she said, feeling her legs about to give way and sagging against the wall for support.

Maybe she'd been staring at those photos for too long. Maybe her poor battered imagination had finally succumbed to lunacy and had conjured him up out of nowhere, because what would he be doing at the other end of her intercom?

'May I come up?'

'No,' she said, her mind reeling and her voice breathy with shock.

'Please.'

'Gaby's still away,' she added as it dimly occurred to her that he might well be here to see his sister, not her, and it wouldn't do to get the wrong end of the stick again.

'I know. I haven't come to see her. I've come to see you.'

Oh.

Her heart stopped and then suddenly started galloping as it finally sank in that he was no figment of her imagination. That he really was here, standing on her doorstep and wanting to see her. 'Why?'

'Buzz me up and I'll tell you.'

Nicky closed her eyes and dropped her head back against the wall. Agh, what should she do?

Her head, which was remembering the way he'd been so cold, dismissive and cruel, was telling her to tell him to get lost, but her heart... Well, that was remembering the joy and happiness she'd felt when she'd realised she was in love with him and the pain and agony she'd felt at the knowledge she was never going to lay eyes on him again. And frankly there was no contest because deep down she'd been heartbroken and miserable and she was so very desperate to see him again.

But that didn't mean she was prepared to forgive him the minute he set foot inside her building, did it?

Nicky took a deep breath to calm her nerves and told herself to get a grip. 'Fine,' she said, managing to drum up a pleasing degree of diffidence. 'You can have five minutes.'

'Five minutes is all I need.'

She buzzed him in and then he was gone and she was hurrying to check her appearance in the hall mirror while constantly reminding herself to stay cool and detached. But it was so hard to stay cool and detached when her head was swirling with questions like: why had he come? What did he want? And what could possibly need only five minutes?

She opened the door and gripped the handle in a bid to

stop her hand shaking. She pulled her shoulders back and lifted her chin and slowly inhaled and exhaled to try and stay calm but it didn't work terribly well because Rafael hove into view, looking dishevelled, pale and not a little wild-eyed, and as her heart turned over at the sight of him and she nearly collapsed with longing she realised that everything she'd convinced herself over the last week, all that stuff about doing fine on her own and not wanting him, was rubbish because she wasn't doing fine and she did want him and she hadn't got over him nearly as much as she'd thought.

Throughout the flight to Paris, Rafael had gone over and over what he wanted to say to Nicky and how he planned on saying it. But now he was here, looking down into her beautiful blue-grey eyes, his heart thundering, his mouth dry and his whole world reduced to this square metre of Parisian real estate and the woman standing in it, every single word of his well-prepared speech shot straight from his head.

'Nicky,' he said, and cleared his throat.

'Rafael,' she said, sounding disconcertingly far more calm and in control than he was. 'Come in.'

'Thank you.' As she stood to one side he moved past her. She was tantalisingly within touching distance and he went dizzy with the effort of not stopping and reaching for her right then and there because, considering the way they'd parted, he didn't think that would be the best move he could ever make.

She closed the door and showed him into her sitting room and then whipped past him and leaned against the edge of her desk, her arms folded over her chest and her expression still utterly inscrutable.

What with the overall chilliness of her demeanour Rafael got the impression that she wasn't entirely happy to see him, but that was fine. That was what he'd expected and he was ready for it. Besides, he was fired up and on an unstoppable mission, in love with her and totally prepared to fight for her.

'So how have you been?' he said, shoving his hands in his pockets because they'd suddenly started shaking a little.

'Absolutely fine,' she said with a cool smile. 'You?'

'Grumpy as hell.'

'Oh?' she said, arching an eyebrow. 'What happened?' Before he could answer she held up a hand and flashed him a tight smile. 'No, no, don't tell me. Let me guess. One of your precious plants died.' Ruthlessly ignoring her sardonic tone, Rafael slowly shook his head. 'No? OK, then, your latest batch of wine is undrinkable? Or hang on, I know, someone actually dared to ask you for advice.'

Her sarcasm was nothing less than he deserved, and he told himself that if she really hadn't wanted to see him she'd never have let him in, and if she really no longer cared she wouldn't be trying so hard to pretend she didn't. At least he hoped to God that was the case. 'Something infinitely more troubling than any of that,' he said.

'Excellent.'

'How's work?' he asked, wondering if a sudden change in direction might crack her unpromising and actually faintly disconcerting façade.

But Nicky didn't bat an eyelid. 'Fantastic,' she said smoothly. 'I've been looking at diversifying.'

'Into what?'

'All sorts of things. Corporate stuff. Social events. The odd wedding and christening.'

Rafael tilted his head. 'That's quite a change.'

'A necessary one. What with all that travel my carbon footprint was getting way too big and my previous subject matter had begun to pall.'

'I remember.'

She arched that eyebrow once again. 'I'm surprised.'

'I remember it all.'

She went pink and her gaze slid over his shoulder. 'That's unforgivable,' she muttered and bit on her lip.

Rafael glanced around to see what was suddenly of such interest and as he did so he clocked the pictures on the walls, the cushions strewn over the sofa and armchairs, and what he could only describe as clutter littering the place.

Hadn't she told him once that her flat was only a rental? That she'd never bothered filling it as she didn't know how long she'd be staying? None of what he could see right now looked particularly temporary.

'Nice place,' he murmured, feeling a bit derailed by the knowledge.

'Yes, well, I decided if I'm going to settle down here then I might as well put some effort into it.'

He frowned. 'Settle down here?'

'That's right. I'm buying the flat off my landlord.'

She sounded so matter-of-fact, so sorted, it suddenly struck him that he might have left it too late after all and he went cold. 'Right,' he said as the room spun for a second. 'I see. Right. Congratulations.'

'Thanks. Is there a problem?'

'No problem.' He shoved a hand through his hair and told himself to stay focused. 'It's just something of a surprise to discover that someone who's always claimed to be rootless wants to put down after roots after all.' And without him.

'Well, why not?' she said indignantly. 'I'm twenty-nine. I can't drift around for ever.'

'This is true.'

'I need to start thinking about the future. You know, pensions and stuff.'

'Sensible.'

'It's normal.'

'It is.'

'So why the surprise?' Her expression cleared and she let out a little laugh. 'Oh, I get it. You expected to find me huddled in a pathetic heap, weeping buckets over you, didn't you?'

'No,' he said, because he hadn't. Although to be honest he hadn't expected to find her quite so together either.

'Why are you here, Rafael?' she said with a sudden weariness that for some reason scared the living daylights out of him. 'Surely it can't be to admire my interior-decorating skills.'

'It isn't.'

'And it can't be out of any concern for my welfare.'

'Can't it?'

'You of all people know it can't. So?'

She set her hands on her hips and glared at him and Rafael pulled himself together. However she felt about him now—and he *really* didn't want to contemplate the notion he'd managed to kill off her love for good back there in his car—the least she deserved was an explanation for his abominable behaviour the last time they'd seen each other. Taking a deep breath, he stuck his hands in the back pockets of his jeans and said, 'I came to tell you about my plants.'

Nicky really wished Rafael hadn't done that thing with his hands because up until that point she'd been doing so well.

Deeply concerned by the realisation that she still loved him as much as she ever had, she'd decided that channelling her inner ice queen was the way to handle his sudden heart-stopping appearance on her doorstep, and in her mind's eye she'd been standing there wearing a white dress encrusted with icicles, a vast pointy ruff made of glass round her neck and a white bouffant wig studded with a thousand tiny glittering crystals. She'd even mentally added a touch of white powder to her face and white lipstick to her mouth, and to her delight she'd had the feeling that he'd found her frostiness a bit uncomfortable. A little unsettling. And rather unexpected.

But then he'd stuck his hands in his pockets and it instantly dragged her attention away from all things ice and made it settle firstly on the stretched shirt behind which lay his chest, and then lower on the stretched jeans, behind which lay—

As heat blasted through her and incinerated the ice Nicky snapped her gaze back up and swallowed hard as she determinedly put all thoughts of his lovely warm body out of her head and concentrated on not giving in to her pathetically weak resistance and flinging herself into his arms.

'Your plants?' she echoed, hoping her disdain masked her sudden light-headedness. 'You came all the way to Paris to tell me about your plants? Why on earth would I want to know about your plants? What do they have to do with anything?'

'Very possibly, nothing.' He glanced up at the clock solemnly ticking away on the wall and gave her a faint smile that was most definitely *not* making the ice chips surrounding her heart melt. 'But I still have three minutes left.'

She frowned, momentarily distracted by his mouth. 'What?'

'You gave me five minutes. There are three left.'

So she had. 'Of course,' she said with an airy wave of her hand. 'Well, if you want to use them to talk about your plants, be my guest.'

Rafael tilted his head and stared at her for a few long seconds during which it seemed to Nicky that all she could hear was the apparently thunderous beat of her heart and the rasp of her breathing.

'You were absolutely right, you know,' he said eventually.

'About what?'

'Everything.'

Nicky blinked and went still because he'd suddenly gone all dark and serious and it was doing crazy things to her pulse. 'Everything?'

He nodded. 'Everything. I *do* back off whenever the going gets tough.'

'Oh.'

'Yes.' He rubbed a hand along his jaw but all that did was make her think about the times *she'd* run her hand along his jaw and how much she longed to do it again. 'I've been thinking about it and I reckon I probably picked it up from my father.'

'Your father?'

Rafael nodded. 'It's the way he deals with things. He's an academic. Linguistics. Anyway, whenever things get too overwhelming he buries himself in his study with his books.'

'I see,' she said, although frankly she was struggling to see anything other than him.

'And I have my roof terrace and my plants, my vineyard and my vines.' He shoved his hands through his hair, shifted his weight from one foot to the other and cleared his throat. 'Remember how I told you about the time when I stopped letting my sisters bother me?'

'Vaguely,' she said, because she wasn't about to confess that she'd been over every conversation they'd ever had so often that at times she'd wanted to tear her hair out.

'Well, before that, whenever things got too much I used to run to the end of the garden and take refuge there. It was my sanctuary. I used to—ah—talk to the trees and make up imaginary worlds where girls didn't exist...' He winced and she couldn't help melting just that little bit more at the way he was going through with all this even though it was clearly mortifying him. Then he took a deep breath. 'I guess growing up as the only boy among four sisters taught me that emotion is a weakness and one that can all too easily be exploited.' He gave her a faint smile and her stupidly fragile heart squeezed. 'Certainly boarding school didn't change that perception and in the end I became adept at not giving a damn. I told myself that life's a lot easier if you simply don't care about things. About people.'

Nicky swallowed hard in an effort to suppress all the emotions that were about to spring free from their confines, but she had the feeling that she was losing the battle. 'Sometimes you don't have a choice.'

He stared at her intently, his eyes burning into hers. 'No.' And then he shrugged. 'So there you have it,' he said with a small self-deprecating smile. 'I *am* an emotional coward. When you told me you loved me it spooked the hell out of me. I'd just realised that you made me feel things I'd never felt before and hadn't ever wanted to. We'd just had that conversation about Marina and all I could think about was how dependent on me she'd become, how manipulative she'd been and how horribly it all ended. I reacted horrifically and for that there's no excuse.'

And he sounded so flat, so bleak and resigned that suddenly everything she'd been trying to hold down spilled over. 'No,' she said fiercely, her heart racing and her throat aching. 'I was wrong.'

'You weren't.' He rubbed a hand over his face and then his entire body shuddered. 'But, God, Nicky, I'm sorry for letting you leave like that.'

And when his hand dropped and she saw the tormented expression on his face, the anguish in his eyes and heard the raw honesty in his voice, Nicky felt what was left of her pseudo-steeliness crumble. 'No, *I'm* sorry,' she said, her voice croaky and shaky with the rush of emotion. 'I should never have said any of it.'

'Yes, you should.' He raked his hands through his hair. 'I needed to hear it.'

'I was out of line.'

'You had every reason to be.'

'No, I didn't.'

'You did.' He stared at her, his eyes suddenly clear and focused absolutely on her. 'You don't back down from any-thing, do you?' he said with what sounded like awed won-der. 'You face everything head-on.'

Nicky swallowed down the lump that had suddenly lodged in her throat. 'I've never seen the point of not doing that.'

'You know, you're the bravest woman I've ever met.' His expression softened and the look in his eyes made her heart lurch madly.

'No, I'm not. I'm a mess. I can't even bump into someone without going loopy.' She unfolded her arms and gripped the edges of the desk just in case her knees actually did give way.

He began to walk towards her and with every step he took she became a little more breathless. 'You're beautiful.'

'You're insane,' she murmured as he stopped just in front of her, overwhelming her senses and scattering her wits.

'I'm certainly crazy about you.'

'What?' she breathed, her heart galloping and the awful tension inside her making her go a bit dizzy.

'Nicky, I love you.'

And then the world shuddered to a halt and time stopped altogether because she'd wanted it so badly, had wanted *so* much for this to be why he'd come, and she'd tried so hard not to let herself hope, and now she didn't have to.

'Really?' she said giddily.

'Really.'

'But I thought you only did lust.'

'So did I.' He put his hands on her upper arms and she felt herself tremble with longing. 'But that was another thing you were right about. I've been stupidly deluded this past week because how could I not be in love with you? You're incred-

ible. Mind-blowingly gorgeous. Supremely talented and utterly fearless.' He looked down at her, his eyes blazing so
fiercely that she could barely breathe. 'You completely dazzle
me, Nicky. You make me want to experience every emotion
under the sun. I'm sorry I've been such a thick-headed idiot
for not realising it before, and I know how badly I hurt you,
but maybe if you'd let me stick around for a while I could
try and make it up to you.'

'How long are we talking?'

'Seventy years, give or take a few.'

'That sounds like a long time.'

He frowned. 'Too long for you?'

And then finally she let loose everything that had been
caught up inside her and was suddenly grinning like a fool
as love and heat and happiness poured through her. 'Not
nearly long enough because I love you too.'

He dragged her into his arms as if he never wanted to let
her go and buried his face in her hair. 'Thank God for that,'
he muttered. 'Thank *God*.'

And then he drew back and cupped her face and kissed
her until she couldn't think straight. By the time he pulled
back, his breathing was as ragged as hers and his heart was
banging frantically against hers.

'I know you're perfectly capable of looking after yourself,' he said, keeping her wrapped in his arms as he looked
down at her, the love shining in his eyes almost stealing her
breath, 'but do you think you might be able to lean on me
from time to time?'

She tilted her head and grinned up at him as she pretended
to consider. 'I should think that could probably be arranged.'

'And if you ever need advice or help or anything, in fact,
might you think of asking me?'

'Only if you promise to do the same.'

'I do.'

She gave him a cheeky smile. 'Good, because frankly you could do with the help.'

'I know.'

Her smile wobbled for a second. 'And actually I could do with some too.'

He held her tighter and she could feel his strength surrounding her. 'Whatever you need.'

'I just need you.'

'You have me.'

Her heart swelled with everything she felt and her eyes stung. 'You should probably know,' she said shakily, 'I'm hopeless at relationships.'

'So am I.'

'I haven't even had a proper one.'

'Well, I've only really tried it once and it didn't exactly work out well.'

She shook her head in bemusement. 'So what on earth do we think we're letting ourselves in for?'

Rafael grinned and lifted her onto the desk. 'I have absolutely no idea. All I do know is that I can't think of anywhere else I'd rather be than with you and I can't think of anything else I'd rather be doing.'

He looked down at her, his eyes shining with love and the promise of a lifetime of happiness, and somehow she knew they'd be fine. Smiling up at him, she wound her arms round his neck and pulled him down and murmured against his mouth, 'Neither can I.'

* * * * *

Mills & Boon® Hardback

May 2013

ROMANCE

A Rich Man's Whim	Lynne Graham
A Price Worth Paying?	Trish Morey
A Touch of Notoriety	Carole Mortimer
The Secret Casella Baby	Cathy Williams
Maid for Montero	Kim Lawrence
Captive in his Castle	Chantelle Shaw
Heir to a Dark Inheritance	Maisey Yates
A Legacy of Secrets	Carol Marinelli
Her Deal with the Devil	Nicola Marsh
One More Sleepless Night	Lucy King
A Father for Her Triplets	Susan Meier
The Matchmaker's Happy Ending	Shirley Jump
Second Chance with the Rebel	Cara Colter
First Comes Baby...	Michelle Douglas
Anything but Vanilla...	Liz Fielding
It was Only a Kiss	Joss Wood
Return of the Rebel Doctor	Joanna Neil
One Baby Step at a Time	Meredith Webber

MEDICAL

NYC Angels: Flirting with Danger	Tina Beckett
NYC Angels: Tempting Nurse Scarlet	Wendy S. Marcus
One Life Changing Moment	Lucy Clark
P.S. You're a Daddy!	Dianne Drake

Mills & Boon® Large Print

May 2013

ROMANCE

Beholden to the Throne	Carol Marinelli
The Petrelli Heir	Kim Lawrence
Her Little White Lie	Maisey Yates
Her Shameful Secret	Susanna Carr
The Incorrigible Playboy	Emma Darcy
No Longer Forbidden?	Dani Collins
The Enigmatic Greek	Catherine George
The Heir's Proposal	Raye Morgan
The Soldier's Sweetheart	Soraya Lane
The Billionaire's Fair Lady	Barbara Wallace
A Bride for the Maverick Millionaire	Marion Lennox

HISTORICAL

Some Like to Shock	Carole Mortimer
Forbidden Jewel of India	Louise Allen
The Caged Countess	Joanna Fulford
Captive of the Border Lord	Blythe Gifford
Behind the Rake's Wicked Wager	Sarah Mallory

MEDICAL

Maybe This Christmas...?	Alison Roberts
A Doctor, A Fling & A Wedding Ring	Fiona McArthur
Dr Chandler's Sleeping Beauty	Melanie Milburne
Her Christmas Eve Diamond	Scarlet Wilson
Newborn Baby For Christmas	Fiona Lowe
The War Hero's Locked-Away Heart	Louisa George

Mills & Boon® Hardback
June 2013

ROMANCE

The Sheikh's Prize	Lynne Graham
Forgiven but not Forgotten?	Abby Green
His Final Bargain	Melanie Milburne
A Throne for the Taking	Kate Walker
Diamond in the Desert	Susan Stephens
A Greek Escape	Elizabeth Power
Princess in the Iron Mask	Victoria Parker
An Invitation to Sin	Sarah Morgan
Too Close for Comfort	Heidi Rice
The Right Mr Wrong	Natalie Anderson
The Making of a Princess	Teresa Carpenter
Marriage for Her Baby	Raye Morgan
The Man Behind the Pinstripes	Melissa McClone
Falling for the Rebel Falcon	Lucy Gordon
Secrets & Saris	Shoma Narayanan
The First Crush Is the Deepest	Nina Harrington
One Night She Would Never Forget	Amy Andrews
When the Cameras Stop Rolling...	Connie Cox

MEDICAL

NYC Angels: Making the Surgeon Smile	Lynne Marshall
NYC Angels: An Explosive Reunion	Alison Roberts
The Secret in His Heart	Caroline Anderson
The ER's Newest Dad	Janice Lynn

0513 GEN STD HB

Mills & Boon® Large Print

June 2013

ROMANCE

Sold to the Enemy	Sarah Morgan
Uncovering the Silveri Secret	Melanie Milburne
Bartering Her Innocence	Trish Morey
Dealing Her Final Card	Jennie Lucas
In the Heat of the Spotlight	Kate Hewitt
No More Sweet Surrender	Caitlin Crews
Pride After Her Fall	Lucy Ellis
Her Rocky Mountain Protector	Patricia Thayer
The Billionaire's Baby SOS	Susan Meier
Baby out of the Blue	Rebecca Winters
Ballroom to Bride and Groom	Kate Hardy

HISTORICAL

Never Trust a Rake	Annie Burrows
Dicing with the Dangerous Lord	Margaret McPhee
Haunted by the Earl's Touch	Ann Lethbridge
The Last de Burgh	Deborah Simmons
A Daring Liaison	Gail Ranstrom

MEDICAL

From Christmas to Eternity	Caroline Anderson
Her Little Spanish Secret	Laura Iding
Christmas with Dr Delicious	Sue MacKay
One Night That Changed Everything	Tina Beckett
Christmas Where She Belongs	Meredith Webber
His Bride in Paradise	Joanna Neil

0513 GEN STD LP